The Pacts Of M&M may be ordered via the internet on:

www.Amazon.com

www.NafessaCollins.com

First Printing 2023

Mrs. Precious Books, Philadelphia, PA 19128

Book Design & Cover Illustration by Nafessa Collins

ISBN 978-0-9963774-4-7

Printed in the United States of America

Acknowledgments

I want to thank God for allowing me to be! Thank You, G, A, A, Mo-E., & O, for ALL that YOU ARE… ALL that you do… and for BEING!

"I am free… Free of all that old shit! Free of all the old ways of doing & thinking! Free!

I am who I am… and I am happy with who I am. I feel what I feel. I am pleased & at peace with what I feel. I am a thinking woman who knows … and I'm cool with that. I am Free… I am Nafessa… and that's all I need to be… me.!"

~Nafessa Collins~

Thank YOU, reader… for reading!

Peace & Love… Always!

The Pacts of M & M

Chapter 1 - From the Gas Station to Brunch

Mackenzie was all ready to go to the club; she just had to get some gas first! She headed for the parkway over by 52nd Street. While driving on 52nd Street, she stopped at the A-Plus gas station on 52nd & Spruce Street.

As she drove her Yukon Denali to one of the gas pumps, a man was just standing there as if he worked there. He wasn't standing next to a car; he was just standing there by himself! Mackenzie drove her truck closer to the pump and near the strange, but handsome, man. She put her foot on the brake, smiled, and stuck her head out of the window toward him. "Are you ready to go? C'mon," she said, laughing. The handsome man laughed right along with Mackenzie. She quickly put the truck in park, rolled up her window, grabbed her purse, snatched the key from the ignition, and opened the door.

"Here, let me help you with that," the man said, assisting her with the door.

"Why thank you Mr...."

"Miguel," he said, offering his hand in a kind gesture, "You're welcome Mrs...."

Mackenzie held her hand out. "Mackenzie and it's just Ms."

Miguel closed the door. "It's nice to meet you, Mackenzie. You look beautiful!"

Mackenzie smiled! "Thank you, Miguel!"

Miguel respectfully looked at her from head to toe. "Where are you headed tonight, looking like that?"

Mackenzie quickly glanced at his entire presence and slightly tilted her head to the side. "I'm headed downtown to meet up with some friends and then dancing."

"Oh! Girl's night out, huh?"

"Yeah, you know it," she said, laughing. Mackenzie walked toward the mini market so that she could pay for her gas.

She thought for a minute and turned back toward where Miguel was standing. "By the way, why are you standing out here all alone on a Friday night, looking all fine?"

Miguel shook his head and laughed. "I'm meeting someone here."

Mackenzie assumed he was waiting for a female friend. "Oh, ok! Well, enjoy yourself tonight and be safe."

Miguel smiled, "I will. You too!"

"Thanks!" Mackenzie walked inside and stood in line to pay for her gas. There were six people in line, and she was number six! Mackenzie patiently looked around the store, wondering if she should buy some gum when she spotted him! Miguel, along with three other men behind him, entered the store. Mackenzie smiled and tried to pay him no attention until he stood in line right behind her.

Miguel slowly leaned toward Mackenzie's body. "You smell amazing! What do you have on if you don't mind me asking?"

Mackenzie turned her head around and smiled at him. "It's that new Febreze scent mixed with some Fabulosa!"

Miguel laughed as he inched closer to her body, slightly touching her. "I promise I won't tell!" Mackenzie just smiled at him. She turned her head toward the cashier and tried to focus her attention on the line ahead. "Excuse me, Mackenzie," Miguel whispered in her ear. "Can I at least know where you're going tonight, so I can see you again later?"

Mackenzie slightly turned her head so that he could hear her. "I'll be at the Lucky Strike, but I don't know for how long." Mackenzie inched up in the line. There was now only one person in front of her.

He subtly put his hand on her waist, "I'll see you later on then." Miguel then left out of the gas station market without saying another word. Mackenzie looked at him as he walked out of the door.

"Next," yelled the cashier.

Mackenzie looked at the cashier and laughed a little at how she was temporarily hypnotized! "Hi! Can I have twenty on three please?"

~

About twenty-five minutes later, Mackenzie arrived at Lucky Strike on 13th and Chestnut Street. She walked up the stairs and looked for her girlfriends.

"Mackenzie!" She looked around and spotted them sitting in one of the brown leather-upholstered booths. Mackenzie quickly walked over to them. "Hey Mackenzie," Bianca said, "I ordered you a watermelon Martini!"

"Thanks, girl. I am so hungry! What's goin' on y'all?!" Mackenzie sat down next to Bianca.

"Not a damn thing," exclaimed Bianca, while hugging Mackenzie. "We ordered some appetizers to get started! They should be here soon."

"Wassup Mackenzie," said Natalie, taking her turn in hugging Mackenzie.

Mackenzie laughed, "What's goin' on, girl?"

"Waiting for these damn appetizers, that's what!" Natalie inspected Mackenzie up and down, "Girl, you look sharp as shit!"

"Thank you, Nat.! We all do! It's Ladies' Night!" They all laughed aloud and started talking about their week as they waited for their appetizers.

Their server walked over to the booth. Before the server could say anything, Bianca politely took over. "Hi! We're ready to order again!"

The server smiled, "Ok! No problem! What would you like?" Everyone placed their additional orders. After repeating their orders to confirm what they wanted, she nodded her head, "Is there anything else I can get you, ladies?"

Natalie shook her head. "No, we're good for now! Thank you!"

The server nodded her head, "Ok, I'll put your second order right in! Your appetizers should be out shortly!" The server took a couple of steps before she turned back around. "I'm sorry, I have one more thing."

Bianca smiled, "That's ok, what's up?"

The server squinted her eyes as if she was a little disoriented. She then pointed to Mackenzie. "You're Mackenzie, right?"

Mackenzie looked puzzled because she didn't know the server. "Yes, why?"

The server pulled out a small envelope from her apron and handed it to Mackenzie. "This is for you." Mackenzie took the envelope while the server walked toward the kitchen.

Natalie was furious. "What the fuck is **that** all about? You know her?"

Mackenzie slowly opened the small cream-colored envelope. Inside, there was a cream-colored card with a gold *M* centered on the front.

Bianca was excited! "What does it say?" Mackenzie opened the card.

Guess who? I'm right outside the women's restroom!

Mackenzie grinned! "I'll be right back!"

"And where the hell are **you** going?" asked Natalie.

"It's ok! I'm going to the bathroom! I'll be right back." Just then, the server walked over to their table with their appetizers while Mackenzie sashayed to the bathroom.

Natalie took a sip of her drink, watched Mackenzie walk toward the bathroom, and laughed out loud. "Work it, girl!"

Mackenzie stressed her hips so that they could see that she was doing just that! Natalie and Bianca were dying laughing! Mackenzie turned to the right near the reception desk and there was Miguel. He was leaning against the wall with his handsome self. Mackenzie stopped and stared. "Hey, Miguel! It's good to see you."

Mackenzie couldn't hold back her smile, but Miguel was cool as ever while he just stared at her. "It's good to see you too."

Mackenzie walked up close to him and leaned on the wall right at his side. "So, what are **you** doing tonight?"

Miguel deliberately eyed Mackenzie's legs. "I'm not sure yet. What are you doing tomorrow evening?"

Mackenzie smiled. "Right now, I don't have any plans."

Miguel's eyes glared at her body, then at her eyes while putting his hands in his pocket. "Can I take you out tomorrow evening?"

Mackenzie nodded, "Sure! Where are we going?"

Miguel laughed, "You'll see!"

Mackenzie moved in closer and nudged his arm. "So, are you about to leave?"

Miguel's face turned serious. He stopped leaning against the wall and looked at his watch. "Yeah, I'm gonna head on out. I just wanted to see you again before the night was over."

Mackenzie quickly stepped in front of him and gave him a friendly hug. "Well, thanks for stopping by! That was sweet of you!"

Miguel inhaled her sweet-smelling scent. As she pulled away from their innocent embrace, he pulled her in close and gave her a more intimate, but respectable hug, along with a kiss on the cheek. "Here's my number," he said, handing her one of his business cards. "Call me whenever you want."

Mackenzie read the card and laughed a little. "All right, but don't say anything when I call you at five in the morning!"

Miguel smirked but kept his cool. "Have a good time with your friends."

"Ok!"

Miguel gave her another hug and kissed her on the other cheek. "Can you do me a small favor?"

"Yes, what is it?" Mackenzie whispered, while taking a whiff of his Creed cologne.

Miguel pulled her in a little closer. "Can you call me when you've gotten home safely?"

Mackenzie briefly closed her eyes and wrapped her arms around his head. "Absolutely."

He held on to her close, not wanting to let go of her body, "Tomorrow, seven pm, is that good for you?"

She nodded her head. "That should be fine."

"Good night, Mackenzie."

Mackenzie kissed him on the cheek. "Good night! Again, thanks for coming." Mackenzie broke the embrace and started walking away. While Mackenzie walked over to her girlfriends to enjoy the rest of the night and to answer a bunch of questions, Miguel walked down the stairs and around the corner to Broad Street to pick up his car from the parking lot.

Before he hopped on the expressway heading for Jersey, he checked his phone to see if he had any missed calls. The phone displayed Tasha's name. Miguel's face beamed as he proceeded on his way to see a UFC fight over his friend's house.

~ 1:24 am ~

Mackenzie was on her way home and feeling peachy-keen, but ready for bed. She was about two minutes away from home when she thought about Miguel. Mackenzie circled the block, searching for a place to park, and found one by the corner. After parking, Mackenzie grabbed her purse, locked up the truck, walked to her house, and headed straight to the bathroom.

~ 2:05 am ~

Miguel was shooting pool on the boulevard when his phone vibrated. He glanced to see who it was. "Give me a minute. I gotta take this call," he said to his boys while walking toward the bathroom. Miguel reviewed the unfamiliar number displayed on his phone. "Hello?"

"Hello, Miguel?"

"Yes."

"This is Mackenzie."

Miguel smiled, "Hey."

"You wanted me to call you when I got in and I'm in," Mackenzie said, rubbing raw shea butter all over her body.

"Did you enjoy yourself?"

Mackenzie laughed. "Yeah, I had a great time! How about you?"

"I'm having a good time."

Mackenzie looked at her phone. It was a little after two am. "What are you doing right now?"

"Shooting pool."

"Oh, ok."

Miguel smiled. "So, are you about to go to bed?"

"Yeah, pretty soon. When are you heading out from where you are?"

Miguel observed his friend's drinking beer, "Probably in a bit. Why?"

"Because it's getting late."

Miguel laughed, "Yeah, you're right! I should head home to an empty ass house!"

Mackenzie laughed, "Well, I have an empty ass house too and I'm home!"

"Well, you're a respectable woman. You *should* be home around this time of night."

Mackenzie walked to her bathroom, flicked the light on, and picked up her toothbrush. "Why thank you for the compliment."

"You're welcome."

"You know what? I have an idea," she said, opening the tube of toothpaste.

Miguel became excited. He thought she was going to invite him over to her house. "What is it?"

"How about after you've wrapped up your last game, you go home and get some rest. In the morning, we can meet up for breakfast, **OR** I can cook you breakfast."

Miguel smiled, "Oh yeah?!"

"Yeah," Mackenzie said excitedly.

"Ok! I'll take a homemade breakfast any day!"

Mackenzie yawned. "Cool! What time would you like to eat?"

"Whatever time you would like to cook," Miguel said, smiling from ear to ear.

Mackenzie applied a dollop of toothpaste onto her toothbrush. "All right! Just call me in the morning and we'll go from there."

Miguel looked at his phone. "Sounds good. Is this your cell number?"

"Yes."

Miguel walked over to the pool tables and laughed because his friends were making fun of him while he was talking on the phone. "All right, let me get off of this phone so I can finish up this game and go home."

"Be careful."

Miguel stuck his middle finger up to his friends. "Ok, I'll talk to you soon."

"All right. Bye!"

"Bye!"

Mackenzie tossed the phone on the bed and quickly brushed her teeth so that she could get her butt in the bed!

~ 10:48 am ~

Mackenzie was still in bed when her cell phone rang. She fumbled through her sheets, trying to find the phone. After finding it, Mackenzie answered. "Hello?"

"Good morning, Mackenzie. It's Miguel."

Mackenzie stretched her body and rubbed her eyes, attempting to get herself together. "Hey, how are you?"

"I'm good. How are you doing?"

"I'm doing just fine! How did you make out last night with playing pool?"

"I won a few. Are we still up for breakfast?" Mackenzie stretched her body again while still laying in bed. Miguel could hear her body moving against the sheets in her bed. "Are you still in bed?"

Mackenzie laughed, "Yes, I am! Where do you live? I can probably leave here in about..."

Miguel interrupted her, "No. I'm gonna come get you and bring you back to my house so you can cook us breakfast."

Mackenzie laughed. "Where do you live?"

Miguel finished up shaving, "I live in Mt. Airy. When can you be ready to go?"

Mackenzie could see the time on the clock by her nightstand. "Ummm, in about thirty minutes."

"Where you live at," Miguel demanded.

"I live in West Philly, 60th and Webster. I'll text you the address."

Miguel checked his watch. "All right, I'll be there in thirty minutes."

Mackenzie thought about what she was going to cook. "Ok, we should probably stop at the market before we go to your house, so..."

Miguel cut her suggestion short. "I have everything at the house that you need. I'll see you in a bit."

"All right!"

Click! Mackenzie chuckled, "So much for goodbye!" Mackenzie got up and picked out an outfit to wear for this offbeat summer Saturday morning. She came across a nice dress but put it back. "Too much for the first date." Mackenzie searched again and then found a pair of shorts and a tee shirt. She then changed her mind, picked the dress back up, and wore it! Mackenzie decided on a nice pair of sandals so that she could show off her cutie-pa-tooty toes!

About thirty minutes later, Miguel pulled up to Mackenzie's home and wrapped up his phone call. "Yeah, do that and call me later! Don't forget! All right." He put the car in park and called Mackenzie.

Mackenzie was standing in the bathroom putting lip gloss on when she heard her cell phone ringing. "Hello."

"Hey, I'm outside."

"Ok, I'll be right out."

"Ok."

She finished up, grabbed her bag, keys, and walked out the door. While Mackenzie locked the door, one of her elderly neighbors spotted her. "Hey there, Mackenzie!"

"Good morning Mr. Smith! Sure, is nice out today!"

Mr. Smith cackled, "It sure is! It's gonna be really hot today! Be careful!"

"I will!" Mackenzie walked down her steps in her pale, yellow summer dress that hung respectfully low onto her bosom and flowed freely just above her knees. Miguel got out of the car and went over to the passenger side of his black BMW and opened the door for her. She walked up to him. "Good morning!"

"Good morning."

Mackenzie sat down in the car, and Miguel closed the door for her. "Y'all be careful now," Mr. Smith yelled to Miguel.

"We will, sir," he said while waving goodbye. Mackenzie opened Miguel's door from the inside and he sat down. "Mackenzie, you look beautiful."

"Thank you! So, what's on the menu for this morning?"

"You'll see when we get there. Did you need to get a cup of coffee or something to hold you over till we get to the house?"

Mackenzie shrugged her shoulders. "I could go for a cup of tea, if you don't mind."

"No, not at all. Dunkin' Doughnuts ok?"

"Yeah sure."

Miguel buckled up and drove toward 63rd Street. "So, what's going on in your life, Mackenzie?"

Mackenzie excitedly smiled. "Well, right now, I'm trying to turn my basement into a partial art studio."

"Oh yeah? Ok!"

"And I'm trying to keep my flowers from dying in the backyard! I try to work out a couple of days a week at the gym, and most importantly, I'm single with no kids and I have a job!" Miguel laughed! Mackenzie followed his lead. "So, what's going on in your life?"

"A little of this and that. I have my own consulting business. About ten years ago, I moved from New York to Philly. I play pool, ride my bike, hunt…"

"You hunt?"

"Yeah," he said, pulling up to the D&D drive-thru.

"Miguel, can I have a small tea with lemon and sugar?"

"Sure." He ordered the goods while Mackenzie went in her purse to grab a few dollars. Miguel frowned his face. "What are you doing?"

"I was just getting some money for my tea."

Miguel frowned his face and waved his hand at her. "Mackenzie, please put your money away."

Mackenzie laughed. "I didn't mean to offend you or anything! I just don't take things for granted."

"It's cool." Miguel drove up to the second window. The D&D employee handed Miguel the small cup of tea after he paid.

Miguel gave Mackenzie the cup, "Thanks." She swirled her cup of tea and wondered if she was going to have a good time or not. "So, what do you hunt?"

"Mostly deer. I haven't been hunting in a minute, though."

Mackenzie sipped her tea. "So, you probably own a couple of guns, huh?"

"Yes, I do," he said, peering at her. Mackenzie looked out of her window. "Oh, yeah. I'm single too," Miguel added.

Mackenzie changed her gaze and examined him. "What about children? Do you have any?"

Miguel briefly checked the driver's side mirror. "I had a daughter, but she died."

Mackenzie put her hand on his shoulder. "I'm so sorry."

Miguel focused on driving. "That's all right. Are you comfortable because I can put on the air if you like?"

Mackenzie withdrew her hand. "No, I'm fine. This is a nice car," she said, changing the subject and sipping more of her tea.

"Thanks! I see you're used to riding up high in that truck of yours."

"Yeah!" Mackenzie scanned the inside of the car. "But this is really nice! I **know** you turn heads with the females!"

Miguel laughed, "Oh yeah? How can you tell?"

"Because it's fly as hell, that's why!" They both laughed out loud. Miguel turned onto Lincoln Drive, after flying down City Line Avenue, and headed toward his house. It was quiet in the car for about ten minutes and Miguel was feeling a little dismayed. He didn't like the fact that she kept looking out of the window, not saying anything to him!

"Miguel, you know what?"

"What?"

"I know people say this a lot, but it is a nice day today. I mean, it feels so peaceful!" Miguel glanced at her for a brief minute while her focus remained outdoors. "How much further do we have to go?"

"About two minutes."

"All right, I hope you're ready for a good brunch?"

"Yeah, I am hungry," he said, calming down.

Mackenzie bent down to scratch her ankle, and Miguel couldn't help but stare at her every movement as she reached over. He could tell that she didn't have a bra on and got excited. Mackenzie felt her phone vibrating and looked over to Miguel, who was staring at her. "Aren't your eyes supposed to be on the road?"

"I'm trying to, but since you're bending over like that in that dress, I can't help myself."

Mackenzie smiled as she checked her phone. Miguel caught her staring at him while he pulled up the driveway. "There's nothing wrong with looking, is there?"

"No. Not at all." Miguel put the car in park. "We're here." The house was astounding! Miguel got out and opened her door. He gave her his hand to help her out of the car. Miguel had a single-family, three-story home on Pelham Road. It was huge!

"Mackenzie?"

Mackenzie looked at the lovely trees and manicured landscape and was stunned! "Yes, I'm sorry. What did you say?"

Miguel was getting a little frustrated with how she seemed to be distracted. "You, ok?"

"Miguel, your house is beautiful!"

"Thank you! Follow me."

She walked behind him and entered the house. "Miguel?"

He smiled, hearing her say his name with her Philly accent. "Yes."

Mackenzie entered the kitchen, and it was absolutely beautiful. "Did you cook already because something smells good?"

"I made the turkey bacon and sausage. You eat meat right," he asked, trying to hold back his laughter at how he phrased his question.

"Yes, I do." Mackenzie put her purse on the kitchen table and walked over to the kitchen sink to wash her hands. "I don't know why I was trying to call your bluff last night by making **you** breakfast because this is the first time I've ever done this on a first date!" She shut the water off and shook her hands. Miguel came up behind her and put his hand on her waist. Mackenzie turned around and faced him.

Miguel had an apron in his hand, "-So you won't get your dress all messy while cooking."

"Thank you! I appreciate that! I need a couple of bowls, three forks, eggs, milk, cheese, salt, and pepper," she said, clapping her hands. "Let's get this started!"

"Yeah, get started," Miguel said sarcastically.

Mackenzie cut her eyes at him. "What else would you like with these eggs?"

He smiled at Mackenzie. "I'll take some grits, if you don't mind."

"Ok," she said, smiling, "I just need a pot to start the water." Miguel grabbed a pot from a cabinet on the island and gave it to her. "Would you like cheese in your eggs, or would you like them in your grits?"

Miguel walked to the pantry to get the raisin bread. "It doesn't matter, whatever you decide." Mackenzie placed the pot of water, with a bit of salt, onto one of the six eyes on the stainless-steel gas range.

Mackenzie giggled, thinking of what she was about to ask! "So, do women cook for you often?"

"Not really," he said, taking a piece of sausage from the warming oven over the range.

Mackenzie playfully shoved him. "Stop eating the food! You know what? I think I have earned the privilege," she said while opening the carton of eggs.

Miguel frowned, "What privilege?"

Mackenzie continued to explain. "The privilege of knowing your full name!"

"Miguel Jabier Conway." Mackenzie cracked an egg. "And yours," Miguel asked.

Mackenzie cracked another egg, "Mackenzie Leah Davids." She cracked two more eggs. "What happened to the last woman in your life or your last relationship?"

Miguel shook his head. "It's been a while since I was in a serious relationship. It ended because she found out I was cheating on her." He waited for Mackenzie's response to the lie he dished out!

Mackenzie chuckled, "Wow! What did she say? Did she know the woman?"

"No!" Mackenzie put the salt and pepper in the eggs and grabbed the cylindrical container of grits, since the water was now boiling. Miguel carried on with the lie to get some type of reaction from Mackenzie. "She was fucking around on me, too. I just made it even!"

Mackenzie shook her head, took a fork, and poured in the grits slowly while stirring. She turned down the flame. "Miguel, do you have any biscuits?"

"No, but I have raisin bread."

"Ok!" She stirred the grits some more, then went to the island and grabbed a frying pan from the center cabinet below. Mackenzie rinsed the pan off, put it on an eye on the stove, and stirred the grits some more. Miguel just sat on his stool and watched her while admiring her curvaceous body move around in his kitchen. He guessed her to be a size 10/12, 145-150 lbs. "Did you love her?"

Miguel burst out laughing! "No." Mackenzie began beating the eggs fast. She stirred the grits again and bent down to get a lid for the pot. Miguel came closer to her. "What do you need?"

"A lid for the grits." Miguel handed her the lid while standing very close to her. "Thank you!" She turned around, stirred up the grits, and put the lid on the pot. Mackenzie picked up the bowl of eggs so that she could scramble them up in the pan.

"Mmmm, that was so good," Miguel said, sitting back in his chair.

"I'm glad you enjoyed it!" Mackenzie took the last bite of her cinnamon & raisin toast. "This was nice. Thanks for inviting me over!"

"Thanks for cooking!" Mackenzie's cell phone vibrated on the table through her purse. She opened it up to see who was calling. Wayne's name flashed on the screen. Mackenzie calmly put the phone in the zipper portion of her purse and closed it. Miguel smiled. "Did I get you in trouble?"

"No," she said, taking a sip of her juice.

Miguel briefly stood up and pulled his chair in closer to where she was sitting. "Mackenzie, I'm gonna be real with you for a minute."

Mackenzie gave him her full attention. "All right, what's up?"

Miguel gazed intently at Mackenzie. "I'm not looking for a serious relationship right now."

"Ok," she said, sipping more of her juice. They were both silent for a minute while staring at one another as if they were playing poker.

Miguel tilted his head to the side, trying to read her. "You all right with that?"

Mackenzie shrugged her shoulders. "Yeah, why wouldn't I be? That's the way you feel, right? I can respect that."

"What are you looking for Mackenzie," he said, adjusting his position in his chair.

She watched him without blinking an eye because she meant every single word she was about to say. "I'm not looking for anything. I'm just enjoying life."

Miguel nodded his head at how he liked her response, "You wanna go out for a bit?"

"Well...," Mackenzie grabbed their plates, stood up, and walked over to the sink area. She was hesitant about his offer and thought about spending some time with Wayne instead. Since Miguel seemed to enjoy the single life and was clear about his intentions on keeping it that way, Mackenzie figured that she might have more fun with Wayne! "What did you have in mind?"

Miguel followed her over to the sink. "You said it was a nice day outside, so how about we go for a ride?"

Mackenzie thought about reconsidering, "Where to?"

"I'm sure you'll be able to see while I'm driving." Mackenzie laughed while Miguel just smirked.

Mackenzie walked up to him, and Miguel backed up to the island. She leaned her body into his, making sure her breasts contacted his chest as her lips whisked his earlobe. "Stop being a smartass, ok?" Mackenzie carefully eased away from him while winking her eye. Miguel just stood there smiling! She walked back over to the table, picked up the carton of juice, and took it to the fridge.

He came up behind her while the fridge was open. "I'm not being a smart ass," he said as he ran his index finger from her shoulder to her elbow. "I just know you're going to enjoy the ride, that's all!"

Mackenzie frowned her face at his assumption. "And how can you be so sure?"

Miguel shook his head, slowly sizing her up while licking his lips. "Mackenzie?"

"Yes?"

"Why did you wear that dress?"

Mackenzie's facial expression stayed the same! "Why? You don't like it?"

Miguel smiled. "What if I didn't?" Mackenzie nonchalantly shrugged her shoulders. Miguel pulled her close and closed the refrigerator doors. Mackenzie just stood right there! "What if I did like it?"

Mackenzie raised her right eyebrow. "Do you?"

"Yes."

"Well, thank you!" Mackenzie just stood there watching him, not making one move!

Miguel wasn't used to this at all! He knew what she was doing, but it wasn't necessary. Miguel was sure that she wanted him, so he took that extra step! "Can I kiss you?" Mackenzie faintly nodded her head yes. Miguel put his hands on her upper arms and reached in to kiss her neck. She smelled and tasted so good that he started with a kiss but ended up kissing and sucking on her neck while instinctively embracing her with his arms. Miguel heard himself moaning and stopped. He was going to pull himself away from her until she licked her lips. "Can I kiss you again?"

Mackenzie nodded her head yes, the same way as she did before. Miguel took his arms from around her and held her face in his hands. Mackenzie stood there with no emotion at all. Miguel gave her a sweet peck on the lips so that he could just gauge her energy.

Her lips were so moist and soft that he had to kiss her again. This time, he took hold of one of her lips and lightly sucked on it while continuing to kiss her. Mackenzie shifted gears and slowly joined in as they introduced their bodies to one another. Miguel

took a deep breath and tongued her down! Mackenzie had her

hands on his back, massaging away! She felt her body giving in to

him and pulled her lips away. Mackenzie just stood there and

observed him. Miguel winked his eye at her. "Thank you for the

kiss!"

"Don't you mean kisses?"

"Thank you Mackenzie for the kisses."

"My pleasure," she said, trying to cool down.

"Are you ready to go out?"

Mackenzie nodded her head. "Whenever you are. On second

thought, you know what?"

"What?" Miguel hoped she was going to suggest that they go

upstairs!

Mackenzie pushed up on him again. She seductively bit her

lip and tilted her head to the side. "Thank you for the kisses,

especially those on my neck."

Miguel wanted her in his bed so bad! "You're more than welcome! Would you like another?"

"I honestly don't know if…," Miguel went on ahead and kissed her again on the lips. As they kept on tasting one another, Mackenzie felt her knees getting limp! Miguel was about to pick her up and put her on the island when Mackenzie pulled back and stared at him. "Can I be honest with you?"

Miguel wanted her! "Yeah, what's up?"

Mackenzie felt a little awkward and raised her head in the air while shaking her head. "I'm not trying to get fucked over."

Miguel loved to hunt! She was well within his grasp! He knew it! "What's wrong?" She just shook her head no while staying silent. Miguel smiled. "Can I have another kiss?"

Mackenzie slowly shook her head no. "I don't think I can."

"So, you gonna make me beg? One more won't kill you, maybe me, but not you!" Mackenzie stayed silent while Miguel just put his hand out. "I know what I said about not getting into a serious relationship right now, but Mackenzie, you gotta let me kiss you again. Just let me taste you one more time, please!"

Miguel wanted to be inside of her so bad! She was so warm, and her skin was so damn soft! Mackenzie was the sexiest woman he had ever been out with. She shook her head yes again and this time Miguel put his thang down! While kissing her senseless, he picked her up and sat her on the island. Mackenzie moaned, and it excited him even more! Miguel had his right thumb running circles around the nipple on her left breast. He took his left hand and played with her spaghetti strap.

Mackenzie felt him and heard his message loud and clear. She ended the kiss. "Miguel?"

Miguel stared at her. "Yes."

Mackenzie licked her sensuous lips. "If we don't leave, I'm gonna end up laying down on this island, on the floor, and working my way upstairs and I don't think you can handle that right now. So, we should get going." She kissed his neck gently, trying to put an end to their exploration. Mackenzie shifted gears and sucked on his neck, nice and slow. Miguel had his hands on her hips and could tell that she either didn't have on any underwear or she had on a thong. She rubbed his chest and played with his nipples while nibbling on his neck. Mackenzie heard him breathing heavily and moaning. His eyes were closed as she moved over to the other side of his neck. Mackenzie caught herself and stopped. She grabbed his face in her hands and kissed his lips. "I'll be outside waiting for you by the car."

Miguel looked down at his pronounced erection and laughed! "I'm taking you on my bike."

Mackenzie put her hands on her hips. "Miguel, I can't ride on the back of your bike with a dress on!"

"I have a pair of sweatpants and a tee shirt you can put on until we go out to dinner."

Mackenzie laughed! "Oh, we're going out to dinner too?"

Miguel frowned his face. "Yeah, you said you would let me take you to dinner tonight. What? You thought breakfast was a substitute?"

Mackenzie shook her head. "If we're going to dinner, I'm going to have to go home and change."

Miguel continued with his grimace. "Why? You can wear the dress you have on!"

"No, I can't!"

"All right," he said, lifting her off the island. "Let me get those clothes for you so we can roll out. I'll be right back." When he left out of the kitchen, Mackenzie picked up her purse and grabbed her phone. She thought about replying to Wayne's text but decided not to. Mackenzie sent Bianca a text and told her she was doing ok and that she would call her in a couple of hours! Miguel walked into the room while she was texting. "What did he say? -Be home by ten?"

"No. He said the same thing as one of your women said to you!"

"There you go," Miguel said, laughing. He handed her the clothes. "The bathroom..."

He didn't even finish with what he was going to say before Mackenzie commanded, "Turn around!" Miguel turned around.

"Why do I need to go in the bathroom when all I have to do is take this dress off and put the shirt and pants on?"

Just then, Miguel turned around! "How am I supposed to know...." Mackenzie had on the tee shirt but not the pants. The tee shirt just reached about an inch below her behind. Miguel just smiled.

"I guess you can turn around now!" Mackenzie laughed while putting on the sweatpants. "I'm ready!" She placed the dress over one of the chairs in the kitchen before they walked out of the house toward the garage.

Miguel opened the garage door and walked her over to his VRSCDX Night Rod Harley. "Put this helmet on. You can take it off when we get closer."

Mackenzie was worried. "Miguel, please don't go too fast, ok?"

Miguel climbed on, started it up, and pulled it forward so that he could close the garage door. "Why? You scared?"

Mackenzie's hands were shaking as she followed him. "Yeah! This is my first time on a motorcycle, and I KNOW you will not take your time!"

Miguel got off the bike, closed the garage door, and walked up close to her. "Just hold on tight, but not too tight or close."

Mackenzie laughed anxiously! "And why is that?"

"I have to concentrate on the road! You can't be distracting me!"

"Well, I'll try not to distract you," she said, tapping her finger on his nose.

Miguel kissed her on her nose and got on the bike. "Saddle up!" He helped her on, adjusted her helmet, and put his goggles on. "Mackenzie, hold on, ok?"

"Alright!" Miguel pulled off, went up Emlen Street, made a right on Upsal Street, then another right onto Greene Street. Mackenzie held on tight and couldn't help grazing his chest while she laid her head on his back. She felt exhilarated by the speed and in awe at how it felt to fly through time! Miguel drove down Lincoln

Drive until he abruptly pulled over to the right on a graveled road along the drive. He parked and turned off the bike. Mackenzie took off her helmet. "Are we going for a walk?"

Miguel helped her down, got off the bike, and looked at her as if he was disappointed. "Why were you holding me like that?"

Mackenzie's smile dropped. "I'm sorry! I told you I never rode on a motorcycle before!"

Miguel shook his head in exasperation. "Mackenzie, turn around for a minute, please." Mackenzie sucked her teeth at him and turned around as he asked. She was feeling a little dismayed at his apparent impatience. Miguel walked right up to her backside and whispered in her ear, "I need for you to hold me like this," he said, putting his arms securely around her waist. Mackenzie's tension quickly dissipated. "Now, you can pull a little," he said, pulling her in closer. "But not too close and you cannot rub on my chest like that while we are riding," he said, placing a kiss on her neck, "… unless you want us to crash!"

Mackenzie laughed, "I'm so sorry! Can you show me again so that I won't forget?"

"Mackenzie?"

"Yes," she said, turning around and facing him.

Miguel kept on with his stern face. "Let's go before I turn around and take you back to my house."

"Yeah, I guess we should."

"What? Are you getting smart with me?" Miguel inched closer, as if he was going to kiss her.

Mackenzie held her hands up in surrender mode. "No, I'm agreeing with you! We need to go! We need to go now!"

Miguel grabbed her helmet, "Let me put this on you real quick."

Mackenzie shook her head. "I don't want to wear it!"

Miguel's voice became stern again. "Well, you have to wear it until we get closer to where we're going."

Mackenzie raised her voice. "How are you going to make me wear a helmet when you're not wearing one? You have until three to put yours on or else!" She poked out her lips as if she had an attitude. "One, two!"

Miguel laughed, "Ok, ok, I'll put it on! Now, apologize for telling me no and give me a kiss," he demanded.

Mackenzie tilted her head to the side. "What?"

Miguel was adamant. "Now you have to give me two kisses!" She huffed under her breath and sighed. "Three kisses!"

"Miguel!"

He held his hands up just as she did a few moments ago. "I'm waiiiitinggggg!"

"I'm sorry for telling you no. Please forgive me!" Mackenzie put her hands on his face and kissed him. She pulled her lips away. "One...," she brought her face in closer as if she was going to give him another kiss, but Miguel held her back.

"If you give me my last two kisses here and now, I promise you..."

Mackenzie interrupted him with her finger on his lips. "Ok! Let's go!"

They hopped on the bike and Miguel drove down to Kelly Drive. He took her to the Philadelphia Art Museum and then to Penn's Landing. They walked by the water, kissed, talked, and held each other like they had been lovers for years. Miguel adjusted his watch. It was 5:32. "I should get you home so that you can get dressed for dinner."

Mackenzie's eyes popped out of her head. "Oh, my goodness! I left my purse at your house! I'm so sorry! I wasn't even thinking!"

Miguel kissed her neck. "We can just go to Macy's, pick out something to wear and you can get dressed at my place."

Mackenzie took a deep breath, shook her head, and pleaded with him. "Are you sure? I can just take a shower at your place and wear the dress from this morning. We don't have to…"

"Let's go before it gets too late," Miguel said, ignoring her compromising suggestions.

While at Macy's, Miguel bought her a dress, a pair of shoes, and some underwear. As they walked over to the cashier, Mackenzie told him she would give him the money back after dinner. Miguel just acted like he didn't hear her. He pulled out a wad of cash and paid for her things. Miguel felt his phone vibrating in his pocket after receiving the change from the cashier. He pulled out his phone, and the display showed the name Brittany. Miguel put his phone back in his pocket as if no one was calling him at all. Mackenzie watched his every move. "Am I keeping you from anything or anyone?"

"No." Miguel handed her the bag, took a hold of her hand, and walked toward the parking lot.

Mackenzie tried to be understanding. "It's ok if you want to do this some other day. I'll understand. It's ok."

Miguel stopped walking and tenderly pulled her by the waist. "Can I have kiss number two now please?" Mackenzie smiled and put the bag down on the floor. She wrapped her arms around his neck while he wrapped his arms around her waist. Mackenzie kissed him, letting him know she wanted him. Miguel moaned as he finished up the kiss. "Mackenzie, I'm taking a liking to you today."

Mackenzie kissed his cheek and whispered in his ear, "You know what? I feel the same way about you!" They laughed and Mackenzie kissed him again. She ended the kiss by grazing her tongue along his bottom lip. "That one was on the house!"

Miguel smiled from ear to ear. "Oh, so do I have those privileges too?"

Mackenzie laughed, "Sure! Kiss me whenever you want to, today of course!"

Miguel laughed, "Ok, I'm gonna hold you to that!" As they approached the bike in the parking lot, Mackenzie took the new shoes out of the box and tossed the box in the trash. She did this so that all the other items could fit neatly in the plastic bag that she carried on her back like a book bag. Miguel watched her while she was getting herself together and smiled.

Miguel was taking a liking to her, just like he said. He liked how she was smart, funny, had a good job, a house of her own, was gorgeous and sexy as hell! He also knew that she had other men in her life.

On the ride back, Mackenzie didn't wear a helmet, so Miguel took it easy on the road. While riding down Kelly Drive, she rested her head on his back and rubbed his chest. Mackenzie then stopped after recalling what he said about the distraction. He felt so good in her arms that she wished they could ride for a little longer.

Miguel slowed down, made a right, and entered Fairmount Park. He parked on the grass by a tree and turned the bike off. Mackenzie thought he had to pee or something! They parked not too far from the road, but it was far enough from where other people were gathered.

Miguel helped Mackenzie off the bike and then got off himself. He took his goggles off, took her hand, and strolled over to a tree. Miguel guided her to lean against it. Mackenzie didn't say a word. She just looked at him. Miguel pressed his body against Mackenzie and kissed her gently. Mackenzie kneaded the back of his neck while he kissed her. Their tongues were finally reunited!

The both of them tried hard to just kiss, but that didn't last too long! Miguel moved his hands from her lower back to her hips. He squeezed her hips and pulled them close to him hard enough so that she could feel him. When he did that, they both stopped kissing and just stared at each other.

Miguel kept one hand on her hip and the other he placed on the back of her head as he began kissing and licking her neck. Mackenzie moaned and Miguel heard her sweet melody. He pressed her hips against him as he started sucking on her neck. She moaned as he moved back up to her lips. Mackenzie pushed him back just a little. Miguel broke the silence. "Are you ready to go?"

Mackenzie shook her head. "No, but we have to go before we turn into Tarzan and Jane up in Fairmount Park," she said, laughing.

Miguel kept his hands firmly placed on her hips. "I'm sorry! I just wanted a kiss real quick."

"No need to be sorry. I'm glad you did," she said, kissing him on the cheek. She couldn't resist going to his neck. Miguel moaned from Mackenzie not being able to control her mouth!

Miguel pushed her back a little. "Mackenzie?"

"Yes."

His piercing eyes glared at her. "I want you to understand something, ok?"

Mackenzie took a couple of steps away from him. "Alright."

"I'm not committed to any of the women that I'm associated with."

Mackenzie put her hands behind her back and understood, "So, you're not exclusive with any of them?"

"No."

She stayed silent for a moment. "Okay. Are they aware that you all are not exclusive? Are they aware that there are others?"

"Yes," Miguel said, beaming. Mackenzie turned around for a minute and smiled at how beautiful the day was. She thought about the men in her life and just wished that things were different. "Mackenzie?"

She turned around and appeared to be unaffected by his honesty. "Yes."

Miguel searched for any sign of apprehension while walking up to her, clenching her waist. "Are you ok?"

"Yes, I'm fine! -Back to what you were saying."

Miguel's gleam returned. "I was just saying that I have other women in my life."

Mackenzie's smile remained. "I have other men in mine."

Miguel knew she did, but hearing her say it made him feel some kind of way. Miguel frowned his face a bit. "I'm not saying that I'm having sex with all of them because I'm not."

She looked at him closely. "To be completely honest with you, Miguel, I haven't been with a man in about six months."

Miguel stepped back and cracked up laughing! "Get the fuck out of here!"

"Seriously! The last time was with my ex. And all the other men that I've been seeing, dating or whatever you want to call it, they want me but…."

Miguel continued laughing! "But what?"

"I'm not sure about them," she said, walking away from him and toward the tree.

"What's wrong?" He felt that something was off by the way she was responding.

She turned to him, smiled, and threw her hands up in the air. "Miguel, I don't have any drama in my life. I'm an uncomplicated woman." Mackenzie paused and continued, "And since we are being honest, one man that I'm seeing claims that he's falling in love with me," she said, smiling.

"He's probably just saying that so he can have sex with you."

Mackenzie pointed her finger at him. "You're right! He probably is just saying that, but who is to say that he's not?"

Miguel glared at her. "Do you love him?"

"No. I mentioned him because it is *because* of men like him that I haven't had sex in a while! Some men lie and do all kinds of stupid shit just to avoid being upfront and honest about themselves." Mackenzie folded her hands in front of her. "Miguel?"

"Yes."

Mackenzie tried her best to be specific with her question. "The women that you are involved with, are there any candidates for something serious?"

He didn't want to answer her truthfully. "No."

She glanced at the trees again and then to the sky, knowing damn well that he was lying. "Miguel, do you want this to be our last date?"

"No."

"Ok." Mackenzie went over to the bike. "Can you help me up?"

Miguel helped her up on the bike and kissed her. "Mackenzie, you've got the sweetest lips!"

Mackenzie laughed, "No, no, your lips are even sweeter than mine!"

Miguel laughed. "You look good on my bike!"

"I do? The way it makes me feel light and free is what I love the most. I might just buy myself one!"

"Whoa, you gotta crawl before you walk now," he said, laughing.

"I'll take lessons before buying one!"

"I can teach you," Miguel said, getting on the bike.

Mackenzie tilted her head at his surprising suggestion, "That's ok! I know you're a busy man!"

"I'm not that busy. I can have you ready to ride in about two to three weeks."

Mackenzie chuckled, "Ok, well, you get back to me when we can start."

"Alright! We better get going." Miguel started up the bike and Mackenzie held on tight to his chest, then moved her hands to his waist, remembering what he said. He picked her hands up and put them back on his chest.

"Thank you," Mackenzie said in his ear. She lightly kissed his neck and when he turned his head, she kissed his cheek. Miguel turned off the bike and turned all the way around, facing her.

Mackenzie eased her way on top of him. "So, this is our first date, huh?"

"Yes, it is," Miguel answered, rubbing her thighs. "And tomorrow will be our second date."

Mackenzie laughed, "Oh yeah?"

"Yeah, we're going to play some pool and I'm gonna teach you how to ride."

"Oh, ok. Well, I guess I have to change my plans, huh?"

"Yes, you do."

Mackenzie playfully hit him in the chest, "Ok playa, but I know you need to confirm your plans because one of your female friends might need a favor, or something might come up," she said, rising off him.

Miguel pulled her back on top of him. "I spend my time with whomever I choose. It's not the other way around."

Mackenzie nodded her head, "I understand."

"-So, we are on for tomorrow," he said, kissing her neck.

"Miguel, I don't know if I can."

"Why not?" Miguel said with frustration.

"I'm trying to contain myself, but if you keep kissing me, it's going to be a problem and you don't need that." Miguel cracked up laughing! "Besides, you're getting your share. You don't need my little piece over here!" Miguel and Mackenzie laughed hysterically! "I'll go out with you tomorrow evening, Miguel! It's cool!" Mackenzie backed up while Miguel stared at her. "Why are you ogling at me like that?"

"I don't know. I just like how you look at me," Miguel answered.

"Now you're sounding like one of **my** friends! Let's get something to eat!"

~

Miguel pulled up to his house twenty minutes later and turned the bike off. Mackenzie hopped off the bike like a trooper and removed the Macy's bag from her back. "Do I have time to take a quick shower?" Miguel smiled, trying not to lick his lips, but he did anyway! Mackenzie saw him. "Don't even look at me like that! You know what," she said laughing, "… this probably wasn't a good idea! I can get ready at my house, and I can meet up with you for dinner later on!"

Miguel walked up to her. "No. I'm not taking you home. You can get ready here. I'll behave." Miguel opened the door. "Let me show you where you can get ready." He walked up to the second floor and then to the third floor. On the third floor, there was a loft that had an enormous bed, a comfy bay window, a spacious bathroom with a whirlpool tub, and a separate walk-in shower. "There are towels and washcloths in the drawers beside the sink."

Mackenzie put the Macy's bag beside the bed. "Awe man, I forgot my purse in the kitchen," she said, heading for the stairs.

Miguel stopped her from leaving out of the room by blocking her from taking another step, "I'll bring it up for you."

"No, that's ok, I'll get it," she said, trying to side-step him. Miguel quickly grabbed her and kissed her innocently on the lips. Mackenzie grabbed his head and kicked it up a notch! Miguel picked her up and laid her on the bed. He straddled her and looked into her eyes. Mackenzie didn't know what to do. She just laid there motionless.

"Mackenzie, I'm not even going to lie to you. I want you."

Mackenzie licked her lips. "I want you too, but I can't be number three or four and I'm not asking to be number one." He laid on top of her and kissed her neck while she welcomed him with open arms. Mackenzie could feel his strength below and knew he was well endowed! She moaned and sat up on her elbows. "This was a bad idea!" Mackenzie tried to get up, but he wouldn't let her.

Miguel had her trapped underneath his body and he loved the feeling! "I'll make you a deal!"

Mackenzie never heard of such nonsense! "What?"

Miguel smiled. "Let's do a trial run and see what happens."

"What do you mean?"

Miguel gazed into her eyes and stayed silent for a few moments while keeping his body lowered on top of her. He then offered her an arrangement. "Let's make a pact! One week! For one week we'll get to know each other some more, go out, just as if we were together. After a week, we'll decide if this is what we both want to pursue further."

Mackenzie tried to get a little space, but he wouldn't let her move an inch! "What about our friends? I mean, what if you're not trying to see me like that and I miss out on a good thing with someone else who's seriously interested in me?"

Miguel grew more and more excited about his spur-of-the-moment but serious idea. "How about you tell them you're going out of town for a week to help a relative, or you have a major project this week at work that will keep you extremely busy. Tell them whatever you want to tell them. It's just for one week."

Mackenzie squinted her eyes. "One week, huh?" Miguel shook his head yes. "So, you won't see any of your female friends for a week?"

"Nope, and you won't see any of your male friends for a week."

Mackenzie closed her eyes and reopened them, thinking of a potential obstacle to their arrangement. "Mmmm-hmmm, what about talking to them? We have to maintain *some* type of communication!"

Miguel kissed the tip of her nose, "Talking is ok, but we need to be respectful of our week."

Mackenzie laughed out loud. "You're kidding me! Are you serious? You're my man for one week?"

"Yes," Miguel said confidently.

Mackenzie pointed her finger at his chest. "And I'm yours?"

"Yes, you are mine," he said, kissing her earlobe.

"Exclusively?"

"Yes, ma'am."

"No bullshit!"

"No bullshit," he replied.

Mackenzie thought for a moment while she looked at him closely. "Since we're starting today, then next Friday I propose we stay in a hotel for our possible last night together. That way, if one of us is done with it all, they can just leave early in the morning or night. No strings, calls, or texts! What do you think?"

Miguel nodded his head in agreement. "So, we'll stay together at a hotel next Friday, and instead of telling the other person...."

Mackenzie interjected, "Right! No discussions! They will just leave with or without a note!"

Miguel went back to kissing her lips as he slowly lowered his entire weight onto her body. "You and your jokes! That sounds good!"

Ten minutes later, Mackenzie tried to push him off her. "Miguel, wait! We can't do this!"

"What's wrong?"

"With me being your woman and all, I can't possibly make love to you on our first date," she said, cleverly. "I mean, you'll probably think I'm some kind of slut or something if I do that," she said, practically laughing!

Miguel just stared at her and smiled at his new challenger, "Ok."

~

About an hour later, they went out to dinner at Ruth's Chris Steak House on Broad Street. They talked about anything and everything under the sun! After dinner, they drove down South Street, walked, and shared some Hagen Daaz ice cream. Mackenzie couldn't help but feel like she just found her man.

Miguel loved all the silly faces that she made and how she made him laugh! Throughout the evening, Miguel kept mentally comparing his other female friends to her. Mackenzie was far ahead of the rest.

He glanced at his watch displaying 11:30. They were still parked on South Street, finishing up their ice cream. "Are you ready to go?"

Mackenzie leaned against Miguel's passenger side door. "Yes! I am so full! I had a great time with you today! I had so much fun!"

Miguel went over to her and kissed her. He planted his hands on the roof of the car so that one hand was placed to the left and to the right of her head. Mackenzie took a deep breath and waited for him to come closer. Miguel slowly pressed his body up against hers. Mackenzie put her hands on his chest. Miguel moved back as he realized something. "You know what time it is?"

Mackenzie read the time on the clock inside the car. "It's almost 12. Why?" Miguel laughed, kissed her lips, and pulled out his key fob. She shook her head, understanding his implied intentions. "It's almost tomorrow, huh? And this was our second date!" Miguel pressed the alarm on the car and opened the door for her. He hurried back over to his side and hopped in. The sunroof opened, the windows went down, and he drove off!

Miguel kept looking at her during the ride to his house. Mackenzie's thoughts were all over the place. She wondered if she could handle what they agreed upon. Although Mackenzie liked him, she tried to analyze things, knowing that Miguel was unavailable and spoken for by many!

Miguel wondered why she was quiet. "Are you ok?"
Mackenzie didn't answer. "Mackenzie?"

"Yes," she replied quietly.

"Are you ok?"

Mackenzie still focused on looking out of her window. "Yeah,
I'm fine."

"Missing one of your friends?" Miguel asked sarcastically.

"-And what if I said yes?"

"When we get to my house, you won't be missing or thinking
about anything or anyone else." Mackenzie smiled and continued
contemplating while peering out of the window.

She was throwing him for a loop! He knew she wanted him,
but he didn't know why she was acting indifferent. At the red light
on Lincoln Drive and Hortter Street, Miguel took Mackenzie's hand.
"We don't have to do anything you don't want to do."

Mackenzie nodded her head in acknowledgment. Miguel
kissed the back of her hand and turned right onto Hortter Street

while the light was still red. He quickly drove to his street, pulled up

to the house, closed the sunroof, windows, and then turned the car

off. Miguel stepped out of the car, went over to the passenger side,

and opened Mackenzie's door. Mackenzie stepped out and moved

to the side. Miguel closed the door and took her hand. Mackenzie

felt like she was moving in slow motion as she walked next to him

toward his front door. He unlocked the front door and let her go

inside first. Mackenzie took her shoes off at the door and turned

around to see that he was messing with his cell phone.

She put her purse down promptly on the living room couch

and headed for the kitchen. "Where are you going?" Mackenzie

didn't answer him and proceeded to the kitchen. Miguel saw that he

had two missed text messages from Tasha. He stopped following

Mackenzie and viewed one message while standing in the dining

room. Miguel then turned his phone off. "Mackenzie! Mackenzie?"

He heard the refrigerator alarm going off and stepped to the

kitchen entrance. The refrigerator door was open. Mackenzie wasn't

in the kitchen, but her bra was on the floor. Miguel instantly became

aroused and searched for another clue after he closed the fridge door. As he walked up the back kitchen stairs, he could see that there was something on the floor at the top of the steps. It was her dress! He thought about going to his room, but he didn't think that she was there. Miguel went in there anyway to grab a few condoms. Once Miguel arrived at the top of the stairs to the loft, there was Mackenzie!

She was laying underneath the covers on her side looking at him standing near the stairs. He walked over to her and sat down on the bed. "-You tired?"

"No. Not at all. Are you?"

"No." Miguel bent down and kissed Mackenzie on the lips. Before Miguel knew it, he was kissing all over her neck. He stopped kissing and sucking on her neck because he was eager to see and taste her breasts. Miguel took his right hand and let it skim against her left breast. He pulled the sheet down a little and stared at her plump breasts. Miguel kissed them, making sure that he sucked on both for an equal amount of time. He sat up, kicked his shoes off, and pulled his shirt over his head. Miguel caught Mackenzie smiling. "What are you smiling at?"

She took her hands and ran them through his hairy chest. "You."

"Is that right?" Miguel said, taking his pants off but leaving his boxer shorts on. "Can I get underneath the covers with you?"

"Yes." He pulled the sheet all the way down so that he could see her entire body. Miguel just marveled at her breasts, abs, thighs, and her pink thong. He pulled her thong off and thanked God that she smelled heavenly!

Mackenzie felt nervous, and a little intimidated. "I know you're used to women with model-typed bodies. I just hope I can hold your interest for a week."

Miguel chuckled and shook his head. "Mackenzie, your body is beautiful." He laid on top of her and kissed her lips while removing his boxers. Mackenzie could feel his hard dick in between her legs.

"Miguel."

"Yes."

Mackenzie was tense! "It's been about six months. If you're not satisfied, we can cut the week short."

Miguel gave her an Eskimo kiss attentively. "I'm not gonna hurt you." Mackenzie smiled and kissed his chest while he put the condom on. When he finished, Miguel sucked on her breasts and neck again as Mackenzie moaned for more. Mackenzie let out a sigh and wrapped her arms around his neck. "Are you ready?"

Mackenzie nervously nodded her head. "Yes."

He picked himself up and physically entered her body slowly. Mackenzie gasped for air and moaned at the same time. For some strange reason, her moaning excited the hell out of Miguel! Usually, he wished for them to just shut up! Mackenzie was in pure heaven!

After about ten minutes, Miguel had to catch himself before he went on a rampage! "How you doin'?"

"Deeper please."

"Oh, you got jokes up here too, huh?" She laughed as he kissed and sucked harder on her neck and breasts, just like he liked. Miguel gave it to her as she asked, but she kept begging for more!

Fifteen minutes later, Mackenzie put her hands up to his chest. "Miguel, wait."

"What?"

Mackenzie kissed him delicately on the lips. "I'm not made of glass." Miguel shook his head and smiled before he started giving it to her. Mackenzie moaned and hummed as Miguel put his work in! He threw up her legs in the air and over his shoulder. Miguel moaned at how her pussy was tight, warm, and extremely wet.

He was about to come when he saw Mackenzie staring up at him. She was biting her lip, begging him to go deeper. Mackenzie put her legs on his back and pulled him closer to her. She sucked and licked all over his neck as Miguel held on tight to her ass, making sure it was planted and ready for what was to come. Mackenzie moaned louder as she was getting closer to climax! Miguel was trying to go longer, but she felt too damn good! They both were moaning and groaning louder and louder! Mackenzie climaxed, letting out a cry of passion while Miguel came moaning in his tenor.

After laying on top of her for a minute or two, Miguel rolled over and laid next to her. The both of them stared at the ceiling trying to catch their breath. Miguel felt a little weird and couldn't quite figure out exactly what it was.

"Miguel, are you ok?"

"Yes. I'll be right back."

"Ok." After Miguel closed the bathroom door, Mackenzie pulled up the sheet and turned on her side to see the tree outside of the third-floor window. About five minutes later, Miguel walked back into the room with a towel around his waist. He laid down on the bed next to Mackenzie, who was still looking out of the window.

She rolled over and smiled at him. "You're not taking me home?"

"No, I'm not."

Mackenzie rolled over on her side again, closed her eyes, and sighed. "All right. I'll be going home first thing in the morning, then."

Miguel shook his head. "No, you're not."

Mackenzie turned back around so that she could see his face. "Excuse me?"

"You heard me. You are my woman for one week! We ain't got time for nonsense."

She kissed him on the lips. "You're funny, you know that?" Miguel usually didn't do the snuggle-up thing. For some strange reason, he wanted to close his eyes for a bit until round two. What was even more surprising to him was that he enjoyed holding her in his arms.

Chapter 3 – The Steady Knock Down

Miguel slowly heard the morning creeping in. He listened to the birds talking outside the window and opened his eyes. "What the fuck!" Miguel couldn't believe that he slept all night like a baby! He had to at least hit it twice before even thinking about going to sleep! That was a golden rule! Miguel sat up and didn't see or hear Mackenzie moving about in the house. There was a note on the nightstand beside the bed:

Good morning! I had to leave out and take care of a few things. It's now 7:45 am. I should be back by 8:45/9:00 am

Mackenzie

She kissed the letter with her pale pink lip gloss! Miguel shook his head, laughing while he unlocked his phone. He had five missed calls. One was from his best friend Teo and the other four were from two of his female friends. It was now 8:53 am. Miguel pondered what he was going to do for the day. He usually spent Sundays with Tasha, since it was her day off. He knew Cindy was pissed off because she was blowing his phone up while he was out with Mackenzie. They all knew their place! Miguel told all of them how it was and what he expected from the beginning. They either accepted it or not! That's the way he rolled.

Miguel heard a car pull up in his driveway and looked out of the window. It was Mackenzie! "Shit!" He picked up his stuff and ran downstairs to his bedroom. Miguel started the shower and put his clothes on top of the hamper. While brushing his teeth, he walked over to his bedroom window to see if Mackenzie was still out there. He could see her sitting in her truck on the telephone, laughing. Miguel went back over to the bathroom and finished what he was doing while trying not to wonder if she was talking to a man or not.

Mackenzie grabbed her purse and turned off her truck. "All right, I gotta go! That's a bet. Next Sunday morning it is! Alright, bye!" Mackenzie laughed to herself out loud as she hung up the phone with Wayne. Although he was a nice guy, he played too many games. Wayne always tried to act as if Mackenzie was the only woman in his life. She knew that wasn't the case. Mackenzie put the phone in her purse, grabbed the shopping bag, locked up the truck, and headed inside Miguel's house.

Miguel finished taking his quick but thorough shower. He hurriedly dried his hair, wrapped his towel around his waist, splashed on one of his colognes, and put his robe on. Miguel checked his face, grabbed some socks, put them on, and tried not to run down the stairs.

Mackenzie quietly set up her surprise on the kitchen table. She heard him walking down the stairs, but pretended she didn't hear him. Mackenzie smelled his Creed cologne and turned around. Miguel was about six feet, two inches, and the robe that he had on reached to his ankles. Miguel walked over to her and hugged her. He wanted to see if that intense physical desire was still there. It was!

"Good morning," smiled Mackenzie. Miguel realized that his hunger for her was even stronger than the day before! She grabbed his face and kissed him like she hadn't seen him in days. Miguel, who was instantly aroused, grabbed Mackenzie's breast underneath her shirt. He leaned her against the island and started sucking all over her neck. She pushed him back. "You had it on this island before?"

"No, but I'm going to!" Miguel pulled her shorts off, picked her up, and placed her on the island so that her ass was close to the edge. As she laid back, Miguel tore her thong apart and opened her legs. Mackenzie got up on her elbows and watched while he let the towel from around his waist drop to the floor. He grabbed a rubber from one pocket on his robe.

"Damn," she mumbled.

"What?"

She smiled, "Nothing." Mackenzie sat up on the edge of the island and kissed his lips. When she pulled away, she ran her fingers down his chest to his penis. "Can I?" Miguel shook his head yes. Mackenzie guided it inside. When Miguel felt her warmth, his eyes instantly rolled up in his head as he let out a sigh of relief. Mackenzie laid back and let him have his way.

"Miguel?"

He stopped, "Yes."

"Can you get behind me?" Miguel gave her a Ronald McDonald smile!

He stayed inside of her and picked her up. "Hold on!" Mackenzie wrapped her legs around his waist and cracked up laughing! Miguel held her up and walked up the back kitchen stairs. Mackenzie kept kissing him, which meant that he had to stop in the middle of the stairwell. Miguel planted her back against the wall and gave her some right there on the steps! He then stopped so that he could take her up the stairs and fuck the shit out of her in his room!

Miguel made it to the top with her laughing and still sucking and kissing all over his neck. "GODDAMN!" He stopped in the second-floor hallway and planted her against the wall again while still holding on to her. Miguel gave her a little more while Mackenzie kept her legs firmly wrapped around him. He then stopped and took her into his room. Miguel pulled out while Mackenzie slowly released her legs from around his waist.

Mackenzie kneeled on the floor and got on all fours. Miguel marveled at the view of her ass from behind while he pulled his robe down to the floor. When he entered her, he had a feeling that he was going to be hooked! Her pussy was so fucking perfect, and he loved doing it from the back! Miguel had to stop twice mid-stride to keep from exploding. He put his hands on her hips and pulled her ass to his dick while he watched her ass jiggle with every thrust!

Mackenzie moaned! "More!" Miguel went faster! "Harder!" He shoved his dick inside of her repeatedly, just like she begged! Mackenzie moaned louder and louder, "Deeper!"

Miguel fucked her hard as shit, "GODDAMN!"

Mackenzie begged. "More!"

Miguel held her hips tight and kept going. "Oh, shit!" Mackenzie wanted to switch things up. She raised her head and her upper back as if she was getting up. "Where are you going?" Miguel said, slowing down.

"I'm getting up." Mackenzie said in a seductive tone.

"No, you're not! Get back down there!" Miguel instructed angrily.

Mackenzie whispered. "No."

"What?" Miguel said, thrusting his dick inside of her. He did it again, but a little harder. Mackenzie moaned louder and closed her eyes. "Now get down!" She did as she was told. A couple of minutes later, she raised her head and upper body again. Miguel pushed her upper body down with his hand on her back. The other hand was still squeezing and pulling on her right hip.

Mackenzie was at her wit's end! Miguel was ready to burst! Mackenzie let out a cry from her intense orgasm. Miguel couldn't hold out much longer, especially when he felt her insides rippling all over his dick. He heard her practically crying from him, beating up her pussy! She was so tight and wet that he couldn't hang on anymore!

"Awe fuck, Mackenzie. Goddamn! Ahh!" Miguel kept moving until there was no more left to give! "Goddamn," he muttered, thinking she didn't hear him. He pulled out slowly because he knew he came a lot. As Miguel pulled back, he stared at his dick. The condom broke! His heart started pounding a mile a minute! The base of the condom was still on his dick! They split the tip and the sides of the condom! It was barely intact! Miguel looked at her sopping wet pussy! He inspected what was left of the condom and then looked at her pussy again. Miguel got up, quickly grabbed his robe off the floor, and wrapped it around his body with the shredded condom in his hand. Miguel gave her a weak kiss on the cheek and walked to the bathroom.

Mackenzie stood up and stopped him from walking away. She put her arms around his neck. "Where are you going?"

"I'll be right back." Miguel pushed her arms down, walked inside the bathroom, and closed the door.

His words felt cold, but Mackenzie waited a while for him to come out of the bathroom. After waiting a couple of minutes in her nakedness, she walked out of the room and closed the door. Mackenzie ran downstairs to the kitchen, found his towel, and placed it around her torso. She picked up her clothes and hurried to the third floor to take a shower. Mackenzie washed her body, dried off, and put her clothes back on. She anxiously walked down the stairs to get to his bedroom.

As she walked down the hallway, Mackenzie could see that Miguel's bedroom door was open. She heard him on the phone laughing as she walked closer to his doorway. Mackenzie was pissed! She walked up to the opened doorway and stood there until he noticed her presence. While laughing on the phone, he casually glanced over to where Mackenzie was standing. "One minute ok," he said, holding up his index finger to Mackenzie.

Mackenzie shook her head. "Unbelievable!" She walked down the hall and ran down the stairs leading to the kitchen.

"Oh, shit! I gotta go!" Miguel hung up the phone. "Mackenzie, hold up! Mackenzie!" He ran down the steps and stopped when he reached the kitchen. Mackenzie was standing over by the kitchen table, reading messages on her phone from Cameron. Miguel was dumbfounded! "What's wrong?"

Mackenzie locked her phone and placed it back into her purse. "Miguel, what is wrong with you? Why did you leave me like that in your bedroom? I know you get a lot of pussy but don't be treating me like some kind of trick! I thought something was wrong with you! I thought you got sick or something! Then I see you on the phone laughing?"

Mackenzie took a deep breath. "Miguel, I know I'm not your woman, ok? You don't owe me a damn thing! I get the hint!" Miguel couldn't help himself from smiling. Mackenzie smiled back, picked up her purse and keys, walked up to him, and kissed him on the cheek. She looked over at the kitchen table. "I remembered you said that you liked sticky buns, so I bought you some from a nice bakery. Enjoy!"

Miguel was beside himself, watching Mackenzie walk toward the kitchen door to leave. "Wait! Mackenzie, what are you doing? Where are you going?"

Mackenzie put her hands in a praying position. "Miguel, it's cool! I get it! We're good!"

Miguel stood in the way of her leaving. "Mackenzie, I don't want you to leave. I got sick, and I didn't want you to see me like that. When I finished in the bathroom, the phone rang before I could go upstairs." He was telling the truth. Miguel did indeed get sick. He got *sick* from knowing that he came inside of her! Mackenzie didn't say a word. Miguel grasped her hand. "I apologize. I'm sorry," he said, while kissing her hand.

Mackenzie playfully poked out her lips and raised her right eyebrow. "Tell me why I should accept your apology?"

"You should accept my apology because I honestly didn't mean to hurt your feelings. We made a deal, and that's that! Besides," Miguel kissed her on the cheek, "I don't think I'm getting my fill!" Mackenzie tried to pull herself away to go towards the living room, but he wouldn't let her go. He pulled her body in close and kissed her on her neck. "Please," he whispered.

"I'll think about it," she said while making a funny face!

Miguel kissed her on the cheek, "Ok."

Mackenzie opened the cabinet and pulled out a plate to get a sticky bun. Her phone started vibrating, and she went to see who it was. The caller ID flashed Charles on her screen. She was about to put her phone back in her purse when Miguel walked over and pressed the talk button!

Mackenzie couldn't believe what Miguel did! "Hello?" She pointed her index finger, chastising Miguel silently.

"Hey, Mackenzie, what's going on?" Miguel lifted her shirt and began kissing and sucking on her stomach, trying to make her laugh.

"Who is this?" Miguel pulled down her shorts. Mackenzie stepped out of them and ran into the living room. Miguel chased right behind her!

"It's Charles! How you doin'?"

"I'm fine! How 'bout you?" Mackenzie asked, running around the dark brown leather furniture.

"I'm good! I wanted to know if you would like to go to a movie and get some dinner later on tonight."

Miguel caught her and pinned her onto the carpet floor with his body weight. He quickly took a condom from his pocket, put it in his mouth, then pulled his sweats down.

Mackenzie laughed so hard at his swiftness! "You know what? I'm so sorry! Something just came up and I can't tonight!" Miguel let the condom fall out of his mouth onto her chest. He then began sucking on her breasts! Mackenzie moaned a little. "Charles, can we get together next week?" Miguel nibbled on her nipple after hearing what she asked Charles. "Owww!!"

"Are you alright," asked Charles.

Mackenzie tightened up her lips at Miguel. Just then, Miguel grabbed the phone from her hands and ended the call. Mackenzie shook her head in exasperation! "Miguel, why did you do that?"

Miguel kissed her neck and breasts. "If he wanted to see you, he should have called you way before the day of!"

Mackenzie attempted to move him out of her way. "Miguel, I said I would think about it."

"Well, think about it."

Mackenzie tried to get up off the floor. "I'm going to get one of those sticky buns! I'm telling you! They are so good!"

He made her lie back down. Miguel put the condom on, making sure that there was enough at the tip of the condom, "You're about to get sticky alright!"

"Maybe later Miguel."

Miguel laid on top of her. "Don't do this to me. I...,"

"I what?" Mackenzie asked, kissing his chest and neck.

"I gotta have some more."

Mackenzie shook her head. "Don't even give me those horny ass lines!"

"Word is bond, Mackenzie! You got some good pussy!"

Mackenzie burst out laughing! "Probably because it's been preserved for six months!"

"It was tight as fuck last night! You just feel too good inside!" Miguel kissed her and opened her legs wide. "Can I?" He held on to himself, getting ready to put it in.

"Ummm..." Miguel entered her and moved steadily in and out of her. Mackenzie gently pulled on his earlobe. "I didn't say yes!"

Miguel kissed her lips and smiled. "I think I'm getting addicted!"

Mackenzie grabbed his head, wrapped her legs around his waist, and crossed her ankles while the heels of her feet grazed his lower back. "Get addicted then!" He had only been inside of her for about fifteen minutes when he started feeling the urge! He *was* getting hooked! After about five more minutes, he was about to combust!

The way she was holding on to him, kissing, licking, sucking on his body, and the way she moaned while he gave it to her weakened him! Mackenzie put her legs down flat on the floor and closed them, forcing his legs to lie outside of her legs. He winced his eyes as if he was in pain! Miguel tried to hold out, but he just couldn't do it! She was feeling too good! Miguel grabbed her ass and planted it, making them inseparable.

Mackenzie pulled him close so that his whole body was on top of her. She closed her eyes, kissed him, and held him tight. "Take me!" Miguel went faster and deeper inside her. Mackenzie called out his name as her body trembled inside and out.

Miguel felt it coming! "Oh, God!" He was supposed to pull out from what happened before, but he couldn't, and he didn't!

Mackenzie laughed as Miguel raised his upper body. "You feel sick now?"

Miguel wiped his face with his hand. "No, I don't."

Mackenzie licked her lips. "I think we should get something to eat. Before you know it, it will be time for me to go home and get ready for work tomorrow."

"Wait, what do you mean going home? We had a deal!"

Mackenzie shook her head in disbelief. "What does that have to do with me going home and getting ready for work?"

"I mean, if we were together, we would probably stay at each other's house during the week, right?"

Mackenzie thought about what he was saying. "You might be right! Since you have the bigger house with all the amenities, it would only make sense for me to stay here, right?"

"Don't hate baby!"

Mackenzie laughed! "Oh, I'm not hatin'! But I need to go home and pick up some things. I'll get them later on."

Miguel shook his head no. "I don't think so. I'll have to get back to you on that one."

"Whatever!"

Miguel lifted his body, slowly pulled out of her, and just hoped everything was ok. It was!

~

Hours later, after eating dinner at the Brazilian Steakhouse, Miguel took her to play some pool. He pulled into the parking lot at the pool hall, parked, and then turned the car off. "Just a couple of games and we can go, ok?"

Mackenzie searched the inside of her purse. "Alright! Oh! Don't forget, I still have to go to my house."

"What did you have to get?"

"Some of my clothes, shoes, and stuff for work." Mackenzie replied, still rummaging in her purse.

"You know what? I don't think you're going in tomorrow."

Mackenzie cracked up laughing, "You are seriously trippin'! What?"

Miguel gave her a serious ass look! "You heard me! I don't think you're going to make it to work tomorrow. Maybe Tuesday! Maybe!"

"Just because you are on vacation doesn't mean …."

Miguel continued with this brooding stare. "Doesn't mean what?"

"You are so funny! Hilarious!"

Miguel got out, opened the door for Mackenzie, and locked up. He took her hand and walked with her up to the pool hall. Mackenzie's phone made an audible sound, letting her know she had a text message. She pulled the phone from her pocket to see who it was from. Just then, Miguel stopped walking and looked at her impatiently. "Mackenzie?"

Mackenzie's eyes were focused on the text message. "Yes?" The message was from Xavier.

I'm sorry!

Miguel stood in front of Mackenzie. "You might want to turn your phone off in here while we're playing."

Mackenzie took a deep breath, locked her phone, and gave him her full attention. "Oh really, I should turn it off, huh? Not on vibrate, but off?"

"Are you waiting on an important call?" Miguel asked, being a smartass.

"No, not exactly. What is this *really* about? I wasn't going to talk to someone right while you were in front of me!"

Miguel felt annoyed with others trying to contact her and struggled to play off his jealousy. "I'm not saying that. I'm saying that we should concentrate on the deal we made, instead of our friends, right? Especially while we're around each other."

Mackenzie made a funny face, and they both laughed! They both knew what they wanted to say but, they knew it was too soon in the deal! "Wait a minute!" Mackenzie tried to suggest a small resolution. "Alright, how about this? When we are in each other's presence, there will be no calls or texts to friends of the opposite sex."

Miguel quickly clarified. "Presence meaning in the same room, house, etc."

Mackenzie nodded her head and pointed to his chest. "Correct! So, if we went out to dinner and I went to the bathroom and used the phone, is that cool?"

Miguel thought for a second. "Yeah, I guess so. But if we are at the house and you get a call while we're watching TV, you're not stepping out doin' shit!"

Mackenzie cracked up laughing! "So, I guess I won't be able to respond to this, huh?" Miguel just raised his eyebrows! Mackenzie laughed and teased him! "Your friends are going to be mad as hell with you!"

"None of them can be mad! They might be upset, but they can't be mad at *me*!"

They continued walking hand in hand toward the pool hall when Mackenzie's phone rang again. She quickly pulled it out of her pocket and sent the call to voicemail. "I'll put it on vibrate."

"Yo' you need to turn it off!" Miguel said calmly, trying to downplay his irritation with her male-incoming calls!

"Is your phone off? Don't get all testy with me!" She walked up to him, put her arms around him, kissed his lips, and then gave him an Eskimo kiss. "You know you're the only man in my life 'til Saturday!" While Miguel kissed her, her phone went off again.

When they finished kissing, Miguel pulled her in close. "Mackenzie, I'm serious! You gotta put that shit on vibrate or turn it off."

"Ok!" She pulled it out of her pocket again and opened it up. The call was from Xavier who had called just a minute ago. She put the phone on vibrate and put it in her pocket.

The pool hall was nice and laid back. There weren't many people there, but it was just enough for a nice Sunday evening. A handsome man, with a face full of hair, walked up to Miguel and hugged him. "Wassup man!"

"Wassup! Teo, this is Mackenzie! Mackenzie, this is Teo!"

"Hi Mackenzie, how you doin'?"

Mackenzie smiled! "Hi, I'm good! Nice to meet you!"

Teo pointed at Miguel. "You ready, man?"

Miguel opened his arms wide! "Rack 'em up, son!" He then pulled up a stool for Mackenzie to sit on while they played. "You alright?"

"Yeah, I'm fine." Mackenzie replied, winking at him.

Miguel whispered in her ear. "Can I get a kiss for good luck?"

Mackenzie whispered right back in his ear as if they were little kids! "I can't. Teo might tell one of your women and that'll get you in trouble!"

Miguel chuckled! "Teo is my best friend. Besides, he only gets formally introduced to those who are worthy of being met!"

Mackenzie playfully hit his arm. "You are so full of it, you know that?" She kissed him on the cheek and felt her phone vibrate. Miguel heard it buzzing! "Yo, Mackenzie! Imma burn that thing for real!"

"Why are you tripping? I'm sure your iPhone is going off five times more than mine! So, don't even go there!"

"We're not talking about me! We're talking about you!"

"There is nothing to talk about because you're doing the same thing!" She winked her eye at him, lightening the topic. "You got women, and I got men! Now play your game!" Miguel walked away and looked back at her. Mackenzie smiled and waved her hand!

After playing two games, Miguel won one, and Teo won one. They agreed to play one more to break the tie. While they were halfway through the game, her phone vibrated. It was Xavier, for the eighth time! Mackenzie left the room and headed for the stairs to go outside. She opened her phone to see who else had called besides Xavier. He was the man she had been dating for about two months. Mackenzie called him and he answered immediately. "Hello, Xavier?"

"Hey Mackenzie, what's going on? I've been calling you all day!"

"What's up?"

Xavier exhaled noisily! "Mackenzie, I'm sorry. I'm so sorry. I didn't mean to hurt your feelings when I cursed at you the other day."

"It's cool. I understand."

Xavier spoke with a concerned tone. "So, are we ok?"

"Yeah, we're good."

"So, when can I see you?"

"I'm not sure. I'm going to be pretty busy this week. I'll call you later on and I'll let you know."

Xavier grunted and tried to wiggle his way back into her good graces. "Where are you?"

"Out, with a friend of mine."

"Call me later on tonight, then."

"No, I don't think I'll be able to! I gotta go, but I'll talk to you later on in the week." Mackenzie hung up and put the phone in her pocket. She raised her head to view the night sky and took a couple of deep breaths before heading back inside.

By the time she got upstairs, there was a female talking to Miguel across the room. Mackenzie knew she was one of his friends and just sat over by the bar. The woman was pretty, but not prettier than Mackenzie. Teo walked over to where Mackenzie was sitting and attempted to keep things cool. "Hey, Teo, who won?"

"I did!"

"Well, congratulations!" Mackenzie observed Miguel and the woman. The woman was infuriated! Miguel was clearly displeased, but Mackenzie could see that he was emotionally detached. "One of his women, huh?" Teo was surprised to hear her say that. "Don't be so shocked Teo! There are still some women out here who like honesty!" They both laughed. "So, I guess she is one of his steady's?"

Teo didn't reply. He just shrugged his shoulders as if he didn't know a thing.

Mackenzie appreciated the loyalty within their friendship and took a different approach. "Why is she so upset?"

Teo pointed at Mackenzie. "Over you!"

"What, I was outside on the phone!" Mackenzie's face wrinkled up as she tried to put two and two together. "Why did he tell her about me?"

"Yo, Miguel **does not** play with that communication shit!"

Mackenzie tried again. "So, it was just about sex?"

Teo stared at Mackenzie. He was stunned at Mackenzie's candor and just shrugged his shoulders again instead of answering.

Mackenzie glanced at her phone again to check the time. "Not that it's any of my business, but since we are both in a tense situation, how long have they been dealing with each other?"

"I don't even think that matters."

Mackenzie shook her head in disbelief. "That's sad! She is a beautiful woman! She can easily get somebody else! I know plenty

97

of men who would love a steady fuck!" Teo looked at her real crazy-like! "It's true! I do!" They both laughed!

Tasha and Miguel settled down a bit. He tried to calm her ass down and let her face the fact that she was in the wrong. They never had a monogamous relationship. Their understanding, from the door, was that they were going to have sex and go out now and then. Being exclusive was discussed plenty of times and he told her no. Miguel said his last words to Tasha, and she walked away toward the main door, staring at Mackenzie.

Tasha then changed directions and walked over to where Teo and Mackenzie were sitting. Miguel knew that something was about to happen. He yelled while walking toward Mackenzie and Teo, "Tasha, just go home!"

Tasha walked up close to Mackenzie and started talking shit! "I don't know who the fuck you are, but that right there is my man, even if we *are* only fuckin'!"

Mackenzie smiled, trying not to laugh, but did anyway. "Ok." Tasha's face turned red. She took a step closer to Mackenzie and lifted her hand so that she could hit her. Mackenzie punched her right in the face! Miguel swiftly held Mackenzie back from hitting her again as Tasha fell to the floor. Teo helped Tasha up to her feet and guided her outside so that there wouldn't be a problem in the pool hall. Mackenzie angrily pushed Miguel away. "Just make sure she's ok."

While Miguel ran down the steps after Teo, Mackenzie faced the bar and stared at her reflection in the huge wall mirror behind the liquor. An older man behind the bar approached her but didn't say anything. "Excuse me, sir. Do you have anything stronger than soda back there?" He nodded his head, poured her a double shot of something clear, and handed it to her. Mackenzie sat down, took the tumbler, and downed it! "Thank you. I'm sorry about what happened, sir."

The older gentleman nodded his head. "She was in the wrong. She shouldn't have gotten in your face like that."

Mackenzie shook her head in disgust. "Can I have another, please?" He poured her another and placed it in front of her. She downed it and slammed the shot glass on the counter. "I need to call an Uber."

The bartender shook his head with disapproval. "I don't think that Miguel would allow that." Mackenzie turned around and Miguel was standing behind her.

"Is she ok?" Mackenzie asked, feeling the warmth of the vodka spreading throughout her body.

Miguel shook his head, smiling at the man behind the counter, and then over to Mackenzie. "Yes, she's good, but she hates you."

Mackenzie laughed and raised her empty glass to the bartender. "You hear that, sir? She hates me!" The man laughed! "Let me call my Uber because it is time to go!" Mackenzie raised from the stool and reached into her pocket for her phone.

Miguel was livid! "What? Where are you going?"

Mackenzie stood in Miguel's face. "Miguel, you have too many damn women for me to fight off and I'm not your fuckin' wonder woman!"

The man behind the bar smiled and paid close attention to the live entertainment!

Miguel backed up. "I'm not expecting you to fight off anyone! Let's just go somewhere and talk about this!"

Mackenzie shook her head from side to side. "Miguel, I'm not trying to hurt anyone physically or emotionally, ok? This is stupid! We can't do this!"

Miguel stepped closer, feeling that she was about to leave. "Mackenzie, I know what happened was fucked up and I'm sorry! I didn't know she was going to come here!"

Mackenzie laughed contemptuously. "Yeah, ok Miguel!" She winked her eye at the older gentleman behind the bar and playfully pointed to Miguel as if he was a clown!

The man interjected, "I think you'll be in much better hands with this man right here than with an Uber driver."

Mackenzie put her hands in the air and surrendered. "Well, can I have one more, please? One for the road?" The man poured her another while Mackenzie paid no attention to Miguel, even though she was standing right next to him.

"Here you are, young lady!"

She raised her glass toward the bartender, silently thanking him. "Sir, I don't drink too often. But right now, I need to do this. So please don't think that I'm a bad person who drinks, fights, and likes to be with men who are already taken by other women!" The older man and Miguel laughed while Mackenzie gulped her last shot of vodka.

Miguel hugged her. "Let's go, babe!"

Mackenzie took a deep breath and stood up. "Sir, thank you for listening!"

The bartender saluted Mackenzie! "Anytime Mackenzie." Mackenzie smiled at him as Miguel took her hand.

~

Mackenzie looked out of the passenger side window the entire ride to Miguel's house. "Miguel, I'm sorry things turned out the way they did."

"It's ok."

"Did I mess up anything that you were planning to have with her?"

"Hell no! Mackenzie, stop being sorry for nothing! It's all good!"

"Don't forget, I have to go home to get a couple of things."

"Alright." Mackenzie fell asleep until they arrived at her house. Miguel put the car in park and kissed her hand. "Mackenzie, we're here." She sat up, opened her purse, grabbed her keys, and opened the car door. "I'll be waiting right here."

"Ok." When Mackenzie walked to her house, she opened the door, walked inside, and closed the door.

Miguel's phone vibrated. It was Teo. Teo and Miguel had been best friends since Miguel moved to Philly from New York. They were like brothers! Miguel knew he was calling to report back. "What's going on, man?"

Teo was already laughing! "Yo' Miguel, what the hell was *that* all about?"

Miguel shook his head. "Tasha and her dumb-ass being stupid!"

Teo tried to calm down from laughing. "What was she mad about? I mean, it's not like she didn't know the deal! Why was she trippin' like that?"

Miguel checked to see if Mackenzie was finished, but her bedroom light was on. "-Because we usually get together on Sundays and I blew her ass off!"

Teo took a swig of his juice. "That Mackenzie is nice, son! Where did you meet her?"

"Out West."

Teo continued with the review while laughing. "She seems nice! I can tell that she ain't about no bullshit either! Yo! You know what she asked me?"

Miguel viewed his rearview mirror. "What? What's so funny?"

"Yo! She was tryin' to ask me if Tasha was one of your steady's!" They both laughed out loud! "Miguel, your join is a trip, man! And her Mike Tyson ass almost knocked Tasha out!"

Miguel couldn't stop laughing. "I know, I know!"

Teo drank the rest of his juice. "I helped Tasha in her car, then she rode the hell out! What you doin' now?"

Miguel looked up at Mackenzie's house again. The bedroom light was still on. "I'm at Mackenzie's waiting for her to come out so we can go to my place."

"Oh, ok! So, what's the deal with this one?"

Miguel checked the time. "I don't know yet. What's going on with you tonight?"

Teo put the top onto the empty juice container. "Not a damn thing! I'm just getting ready for work tomorrow and that's that! But on some real shit! When I was talking to Mackenzie, it seemed like she was down to earth and shit! For a woman who knows that you have a lot of female joins', and she's cool with that, has to be down to earth, you know what I mean?"

Miguel checked his side-view mirrors. "Did she say that she was cool with it?"

"No, but I'm saying she knows that you have a lot of females and she's still hangin' with you! Check *this* shit out! When you and

Tasha were arguing, we were talking about Tasha being one of your jump off's."

Miguel yelled, "What? Did you tell her that?"

"Man, she knew what it was! Anyway, she said she knew plenty of men who would love a steady fuck!" Teo laughed like crazy. "Yo! I know she got many men on her! For realz!"

Miguel thought about her numerous phone calls. "Yeah, I know."

Teo stopped laughing. "And you know how *we* get when we see something we want! Miguel, you got mad competition!"

Miguel noticed that her bedroom light was out. He then saw Mackenzie coming out of her house. Miguel got out of the car to get her bag. "Yeah, I know. Teo, I'm gonna' call you tomorrow, alright?"

"Alright man, peace!"

Miguel ended the call. "Here, let me take that." He took the bag from her, opened her door, closed it after she sat down, and then put her bag in the back seat. When Miguel got in the car, he grabbed Mackenzie's hand and kissed it again. "Are you ok?"

"Yeah, I'm fine."

"Can I have a kiss?"

"Come and get it." Miguel leaned over and kissed her. He couldn't believe how quickly his dick got hard from just kissing her for a minute!

"How long is it going to take you to get to the house?"

Miguel felt uneasy. He made a U-turn at the end of her block, headed for Cobbs Creek. "About twenty-five minutes. Why?"

Mackenzie inspected her hands. "I need you to do something for me."

"What?" He said, driving down 63rd Street.

"I don't drink that often Miguel, so don't think that I'm drunk, ok?"

Miguel laughed! "I don't!"

Mackenzie tried to think straight despite the vodka! "I need you to be truthful with me. Considering what happened tonight, are you gonna miss her?"

"No."

Mackenzie looked over at him while he was driving to see his facial expression. "Was she good in bed?" Miguel laughed. "I'm serious! Was she good?"

"She was good!"

Mackenzie focused on the windshield. "Are you disappointed that you probably won't be able to fuck her anymore?"

Miguel huffed as if what she was saying was nonsense! "No, not at all!" He replied in an overconfident tone.

Mackenzie felt her phone vibrating, grabbed it out of her purse, and unlocked the phone. It was a text from Xavier,

I miss you! Call me!

Since Mackenzie *was* a little tipsy, she wasn't paying attention to how Miguel was reading the message as well! She closed the phone and put it in her purse.

Miguel felt anger brewing inside. "Everything ok?"

Mackenzie was thinking about the day and Xavier. She delayed in responding to Miguel, "I'm sorry. What did you say?"

"-Your call, your text, is everything ok?"

"Yeah." Mackenzie continued, staring out of the window in a daze.

Miguel was now on Lincoln Drive, headed up to Mt. Airy. "Was that a friend of yours who just sent you a text?"

"Yes." Mackenzie quickly closed her eyes, wondering what the fuck she was doing in this man's car! After what happened at the pool hall, she had a strong feeling that this arrangement was all wrong!

"Was there something that he said that made you upset?"

Mackenzie quickly processed his question and realized that she never said that the message was from a man. "No."

"Well, what are you thinking about?" Miguel asked, trying to dig deep.

"You."

Miguel briefly glanced over at her while speeding up on Lincoln Drive. "What are you thinking?"

Mackenzie stretched her neck from side to side, trying to ease the tension. "I'm thinking about a couple of things."

"Well, what are they?"

Mackenzie turned her body to give him her full attention. "Do you really want to know?"

Miguel took another glimpse at her while speeding, "Yes, I do."

Mackenzie took a deep breath and felt nice and warm from the shots of vodka. "Miguel, the main thing I'm thinking about right now is how much I feel ashamed at how much I want to make love to you right now. You are the type of man that I would *never* seriously date because you have too many women! You're not looking for anything serious and I have allowed myself to be completely open to only you for one week! And yet..." Mackenzie concentrated on the darkness outside of her window and took a deep breath. "All I can think about is how I can't wait until you get inside me! I punched the shit out of one of your friends and all I can concentrate on is thinking about sex! That's some fucked up shit!" Mackenzie laughed at herself, remembering how talkative she gets when she drinks.

Miguel was getting excited as he pulled up in his driveway. He couldn't wait to put her mind at ease. Right after Miguel put the car in park and turned it off, Mackenzie's phone vibrated again. She picked it out of her purse and opened it. It was Xavier again!

Please call me! I need to talk to you!

Miguel saw the message and couldn't help but get upset. "Yo Mackenzie! You need to turn that off for the night!"

"What?"

Miguel was fed up! "For real, you need to turn it off!"

"You gettin' jealous on me?"

Miguel felt his temperature rising. "What? Yo, every time I turn around, your phone is going off!"

Mackenzie raised her voice. "So, what! Your phone goes off too! I just don't see you when you check it! Now, if you want me to do what *you* do, I can!"

Miguel lost his cool, "Yo! Are you single?"

"Yes, I am! If I wasn't, I damn sure wouldn't be here with you!"

Miguel raised his voice a bit. "I just read the message on your phone!"

"Ok," Mackenzie chuckled, "... and what?"

"If you're single, why is he texting you about how he's missing you and all that bullshit? Just be honest! If you're seeing him and you didn't want to tell me ..."

Mackenzie tried to take the conversation to a calmer level. "I am single Miguel. The man who just text me and who has been texting me and calling me all day is a friend who knows that I am a good woman. When we met, he was like you, not wanting anything serious. I've known him now for about two to three months and although we've never had sex..."

Miguel blurted out a sigh of disbelief. He was practically yelling at her! "That's bullshit, and you know it!"

Mackenzie leaned back in her seat and spoke softly, "Why are you talking to me like that?"

Miguel was tired of feeling challenged by her! He never had to compete, and he wasn't having any part of it! "You expect me to believe that shit?"

Mackenzie's mouth was agape while listening and watching his demeanor. She closed her mouth and faintly smiled. "You know what? Goodnight Miguel." Mackenzie grabbed her purse, got out of the car, opened the back door, and grabbed her bag. She closed both of his doors, pulled out her keys, and walked over to her truck, which was still parked in the driveway.

Miguel felt like a complete asshole. "Mackenzie, wait!" Mackenzie kept walking as she turned the alarm off her truck. Miguel ran over to her. "Mackenzie, I'm sorry! I'm sorry! I didn't mean it like that!"

Mackenzie turned around. "Yes, you did. It's ok though. I know it might seem difficult to believe that I haven't had sex in months, that I have two or four men trying to wheel me in, and that I have never slept with any of them! Yet, I slept with you after only knowing you for two days! I understand *exactly* what you meant!" Her stark words completely threw him off his game! "Miguel, I know your situation and we made a deal that I thought was unrealistic but fair! Just for the record, I am not a slut, or a whore and I'm no one's steady fuck! Six months ago, my boyfriend was murdered, and that's why I haven't been with anyone, ok?"

Mackenzie walked over to the passenger side of her truck. She opened the door, threw her purse and bag inside, and closed the door. Miguel felt his phone vibrating in his pocket. "Mackenzie, it's late. Let's just go inside and…"

Mackenzie threw her hands in the air. "What? Why should I?"

"Let's just go in, watch a movie, and eat some ice cream or something."

"Why? You can do that without me! Hell, you can do that with any of your female friends whom you *know*, right? I mean, why even bother with me when you barely have the room and the time, anyway?" Mackenzie took a deep breath and smiled while slowly shaking her head no. "I'm good! You're good! We're good! I'm just gonna go home!"

Miguel didn't want her to leave! "Mackenzie."

She walked up to him and caressed his face with her hand. "You think I'm out there like you? You think I'm fucking my male friends like you're fucking your female friends? I was honest with you, just like you have been with me, Miguel." She started to say something, but changed her mind. Instead, she walked over to her driver's side door, but Miguel got in the way.

"Mackenzie, come on inside."

Mackenzie smiled and caressed his face with her hand again. "We knew this wouldn't work. Right?"

Miguel felt that uneasiness again. "C'mon now. Don't go. You had a few shots. Just come on inside and then…"

"Why?"

"Because I'm asking you to!"

Mackenzie kept staring. "I'm saying no."

Miguel took a quick breath and composed himself. "Mackenzie, I want you to stay."

"Again, why do you want me to stay when you can have any of your friends come over right now and do whatever you want, just like you like it? I mean come on! Just stop! PLEASE! It's ok! Really, it's ok!"

"I'm looking at what I want!" Mackenzie turned her head away from him, trying to think of what to say. Miguel pulled her close to him. "Mackenzie, stay with me." He kissed her lips, "You got me practically begging you and shit already!" Mackenzie shook her head no and Miguel kissed her again. "If you stay, I'll give you a massage!"

Mackenzie giggled! "Oh, is that right?"

Miguel tried harder. "I'll run you a nice hot bath, wash your body, and give you a relaxing massage. You're right about everything and I'm sorry! Let me make it up to you!"

Mackenzie cautiously stared at Miguel. "So, what do you honestly think about my situation?"

He thought for a moment, making sure that what he wanted to say came out the right way. "I believe you."

"Thank you." She said, hugging him. Miguel grabbed her bags from her car, locked his car, and opened the front door. Mackenzie pressed her alarm on her truck and walked through the doorway. As she headed for the kitchen, Miguel grabbed her from behind and savagely kissed the back of her neck. Mackenzie played the role and pulled away as if Miguel was the attacker. She broke free and tried to run up the kitchen stairs. Miguel caught her on the stairs, turned her around, and kissed her lips while tugging on her pants.

Mackenzie escaped his grasp, but only made it to the top of the second-floor stairs. Miguel pulled her from crawling away into the hallway and pinned his body on top of hers. Mackenzie laughed, "So I guess this is how you do all your women, huh?"

Miguel sucked on the tip of her earlobe and whispered, "Never!"

Mackenzie squinted her eyes. "You lie so damn much, get off of me!" She pushed him and rapidly crawled to the room closest to the stairs, which was his bedroom.

Miguel caught up with her and playfully restrained her while she laid on her back. He gave her a peck on the nose. "Mackenzie, I don't know what's going on, but I'm feeling you."

Mackenzie raised her head from the floor and laughed in his face. "Yeah, you're feeling me alright, especially since your main steady has been fired! You look like you want to feel me right now!"

"Mackenzie..."

Mackenzie resumed her role. "Get off of me!"

He held her down tight to the floor. "Mackenzie, I want you!"

She tried to pull her arms from his clutch, but Miguel wouldn't allow it! Mackenzie kissed his lips, causing Miguel to loosen his grip! Mackenzie pulled her lips away and yanked her shirt off. "Show me!" Miguel smiled and went to work!

After kissing, sucking, and licking all over each other, Miguel went to get a condom. He reached into his drawer and didn't feel one. Miguel checked the other drawers and didn't see any! He knew he had just bought some on Friday, but couldn't remember where he put them. "I don't believe this shit!"

"What's wrong?"

"I'll be right back, ok?"

Mackenzie got off the floor and laid on top of his bed laughing at him! "Ok!" He kissed her and ran out of the room while she continued laughing! "Be careful!" Miguel ran down the steps and out of the house to his car. After unlocking his car, he combed through the trunk, and then on the inside of the car. While searching underneath the driver's seat, he found them!

Miguel locked up the car and ran back inside the house. While walking through the kitchen, he heard the water running in the bathroom upstairs. As he walked up the kitchen stairs, he could see light coming from the loft on the third floor. Miguel walked into the loft and over to the closed bathroom door. He knocked on the door and shouted, "I'm back!"

"Good, you alright?"

Mackenzie kept on washing her body, unaware that Miguel had already entered the bathroom and was watching her through the shower glass door. He never felt compelled to join in with his other women. As he watched Mackenzie washing her body, he yearned to be closer. "Can I come in?"

He caught Mackenzie off guard! It surprised her how he was watching her and then asking to join in. "Ummmm... ok!" Miguel hurriedly removed his clothing and stepped into the shower. Mackenzie stepped toward the back of the shower so that he could get wet. She surveyed his body from the back and admired his physique! His back was muscular and toned. Mackenzie couldn't resist being the first to touch. She massaged the water onto his back and kissed all over his shoulder blades.

Miguel lifted his head to the ceiling with his eyes closed while she licked and kissed him on his back. He turned around, and they began kissing each other like they were starving for one another. His dick was so hard! It found its way in between her thighs, rubbing up against her pussy. While they kissed, she moved her hips so that her pussy slid back and forth on his dick.

Miguel backed her up against the wall in the shower and kept on kissing her. "You better stop moving like that!"

Mackenzie licked her lips. "Or what?"

"Something might slip."

"You're right. You better step back." Miguel didn't move, and Mackenzie kept going. While withdrawing his dick from in between her thighs, the head of his dick slid across her pussy. He just had to feel that again. Miguel pushed it back and rubbed his head all around the entrance of her pussy. His eyes rolled to the back of his head and thought of the other night at how good she felt when the condom came off. She held onto his arms. "I'm getting out." Mackenzie kissed him and stepped out of the shower. Miguel hastily washed the rest of his body and stepped out a couple of minutes later.

Mackenzie walked back into the bathroom to get some tissue for her nose while Miguel wrapped his towel around his waist. He suddenly picked her up, walked her over to the bed, and laid her down. Miguel just grinned! Mackenzie squinted her eyes at him while her mind analyzed things. "Miguel, can I ask you something?"

"Yes"

"Did something happen the other day while we were having sex?"

Miguel's heart was about to leap out of his chest. "What do you mean?"

"The other day when we were on your bedroom floor, and you went in the bathroom, did something happen?" Miguel just stared at her because he didn't know exactly what to say.

Mackenzie covered her eyes with her hands and sighed. Miguel pulled her hands away and kissed her. "Miguel, what's going on? Be honest with me. Just tell me if something happened! Please and we'll go from there!"

Miguel shook his head anxiously. "Mackenzie, I'm sorry! I just didn't know how to come out and tell you what I think happened because I'm not even sure myself." Mackenzie didn't say a word while Miguel lowered his body on top of hers. "When we were making love, the condom broke."

"It broke," she yelled.

Miguel's voice lightened up. "When I pulled out, the condom was barely intact."

Mackenzie's eyes got big. "So, when were you going to tell me?"

Miguel sighed hard. "I know this might sound fucked up, but I don't know."

Mackenzie just closed her eyes and tried to focus. "Is this something that happens often with your friends?"

"Hell no!"

"So, this never happens to you? You always wear condoms, even with your steady's?"

"Always!"

"So why didn't you say anything? I mean, I know we're not in a relationship, but you could have at least just told me out of respect and consideration," Mackenzie said, showing her anger.

Miguel got up off her. She grabbed her towel, wrapped it around her, and went over to the window. Mackenzie peered out into the night and knew that this was all her fault and no one else's. Miguel wrapped his towel around his waist and sat at the edge of the bed with his head in his hands. This was supposed to be fun, but Miguel just felt like he was fucking it up! He stood up, walked over to her, held her from behind, and didn't say anything. He messed in her hair, kissed her shoulder, and returned to his embrace. "Come to bed."

"Miguel, this has gone too far! I need to leave. This is completely ridiculous."

Mackenzie took a few steps to leave the loft when Miguel stopped her. "No! Why are you leaving?" Miguel yelled, blocking her from leaving off the third floor.

"This is too much! I need to go home and think about things. Miguel, please move so I can go."

"No! We need to talk!"

Mackenzie stared at him. "Oh, now we need to talk! I told you I was not on any birth control!" She worriedly walked back to the window. Mackenzie thought about the beautiful tree outside the bedroom window and how it just stood all alone outside in the darkness. She shook her head, trying to center her thoughts. "I know we already discussed our health status with being disease free and all, but I *told* you I wasn't on any birth control! Like I said to you before, I do not believe in abortions."

Miguel held her close from behind and whispered in her ear, "Come to bed."

Mackenzie turned to face him. "Did you hear what I said?"

"Yes, I did. Now let's go to bed." He picked her up and laid

her on the bed. She turned on her side and he followed right behind,

holding her until they both fell asleep.

Chapter 4 ~ Fuck It!

~ 3:33 a.m. Monday ~

"Mackenzie." Mackenzie opened her eyes and Miguel was on top of her. She turned her head to the window and could see that it was still dark outside. Miguel sucked on her neck and breasts. He put his hand down below to grab his dick and glared at her through the darkness.

"You have a condom on, right?" Mackenzie asked, getting ready to push him off her.

"No."

He sucked hard on her neck and then moved to her breasts.

"Miguel?"

"Yes."

Mackenzie put her index finger underneath his chin. "I'm not your woman."

Miguel kissed her lips. "It looks like you are to me."

Mackenzie raised her voice, enabling him to understand that she was serious. "Miguel, I'm not playing with you! I'm not your woman!"

"Do you want to be?"

"Miguel, what the fuck does that have to do with anything? Don't play these dick games with me, ok?"

Miguel laughed and kissed her. "I want you to be my woman."

"We can talk about that tomorrow! In the meantime, you can't do what you're trying to do, Miguel!" He took turns sucking on one breast while teasing the other with his moist fingers. Mackenzie moaned for more and Miguel decided he had enough.

He grabbed his dick and rubbed it at the mouth of her pussy. Mackenzie tried to stand her ground, but she couldn't resist! "Miguel, what are you doing? You can't do this! I'm serious!"

"I'm about to make love to you and that's that!" He kissed her, took his hand, and put his dick inside of her. Mackenzie and Miguel both moaned and sighed! He couldn't believe how her pussy felt! "Goddamn!" Miguel held her close with every stroke. She kissed

his lips and wrapped her legs around his back. "Mackenzie, you feel

so fuckin' good!" He was dripping all inside of her! After about

twenty minutes, Miguel couldn't hold out any longer! "Mackenzie,

you ready?"

"What are you going to do?"

"I'm about to cum, baby!" Mackenzie lifted her other leg

and Miguel put it on his other shoulder. "Goddamn!" Mackenzie's

moaning got louder and louder! Miguel was going off. "Fuck!"

Mackenzie called out to him, and Miguel answered, "Here I come,

baby! Hold on, hold on!" He held her close and felt Mackenzie's

insides tumbling over his dick! That was the last straw! Miguel was

going to pull out, but before he could, a big shot of cum came out of

his dick! While his semen shot deep inside Mackenzie, Miguel talked

through it! "Mackenzie, you're mine! You are all fuckin' mine!"

Miguel put her legs down, kissed her, and laid his body on top of

hers. "Are you all mine, Mackenzie?"

"I'm yours for one week, remember?"

"You and your damn jokes! Mackenzie, I want you to be my woman! I want you straight up and down! I'm serious!"

Mackenzie caressed his face and kissed his lips. "How about we wait and see after a week, like you said? You might change your mind!"

Miguel shook his head from side to side! "No, I'm not!"

"You don't have to say this because of the condom issue."

"I'm not!"

Mackenzie kissed him again. "Let's talk about it tomorrow and for the record, I'm getting on the pill!"

"Ok! I can keep doing what I'm doing then!"

Mackenzie poked him in his chest with her index finger. "Only if I let you!" Miguel rose off her and laid his body down beside her. Mackenzie turned on her side and placed her head on his chest. Miguel held her until they both fell asleep.

~

In the morning, Mackenzie pried her way out of Miguel's embrace and went to the bathroom. She saw some of the semen in the toilet and on the toilet tissue when she wiped herself. Mackenzie shook her head and flushed the toilet. Afterward, she washed her hands, brushed her teeth, and did a quick wash-up. Mackenzie crept back onto the bed and laid on her stomach, trying not to wake him.

Miguel woke up anyway and looked at her. "-You alright?"

"Yes." Mackenzie started drifting back to sleep until she felt Miguel's lips on her back. He ran his fingers down her spine while kissing and licking. "What in the world are you doing?"

"I'm making love to my woman!"

"Oh, is that right?"

"Yes!"

"You better stop playing around like that!"

Miguel started kissing and sucking on the back of her neck. "I'm not playing around!"

Mackenzie laughed! "Talk that shit to one of your steady's because I'm not buying it!"

Miguel stopped abruptly. "Mackenzie, turn around for a minute." Mackenzie rolled over, smiling, but Miguel wasn't. "Stop playing. I said I wanted you! All that steady shit can stop!" He was talking to her in a very harsh tone.

Mackenzie heard the seriousness in his voice and saw it on his face. "I'm not playing games. Miguel, you have a lot of women! I just met you a few days ago..."

Miguel stared at her, "And so what?! I can't mean what I'm saying because of *that*? Oh, it's ok for you to have sex with me in a short amount of time, but for me to say that I want you to be mine is crazy?"

Mackenzie opened her mouth to respond, then closed her mouth. She was silent for a moment, reflecting on what he said. Mackenzie scratched her head. "You have a point. Maybe you're right."

Miguel laughed victoriously! "I know I'm right! Now, what's the deal? Are you gonna' be mine or what?"

Mackenzie played with the hair on his chest. "I still think that we should wait out this week! I mean, if you're serious about what you're saying," she climbed on top of him and started kissing him on the neck, "you're going to need this time to wrap up loose ends." Mackenzie moved down his chest and sucked on his nipples. "Plus, we need to spend more time getting to know each other better!" Mackenzie kissed his stomach and saw that his dick was rock hard! She kissed and licked all the way back up to his neck and then to his lips. Miguel pulled her forward, signaling her to get on top, but she ignored his signals. "What's wrong?"

"Get on top of me."

"I am on top of you."

He pulled her head down to his and kissed her. "Ride me, baby."

While Miguel kissed her, she took hold of his dick. He moaned, anticipating her next move. "Miguel, after tonight, that's it no more." Mackenzie directed, adjusting to his length.

"Goddamn Mackenzie! You feel so fucking good!"

"Did you hear what I said?"

"Mmmm. -About what, baby?"

"This is it!" Miguel just laid back, holding Mackenzie's waist with his eyes closed. Mackenzie was in heaven herself! It had been a while since she'd been on top, but given the way Miguel felt inside of her, you would have thought she was Vanessa Del Rio's protégé! She rode the hell out of Miguel to where he had to ask her to slow down twice! "Miguel, I'm not playing. Tonight, is the last night of this!"

He sat all the way up with her still on top and moved to the edge of the bed so that his legs dangled off the sides. "What are you talking about?" Miguel grabbed her right breast and sloppily sucked all over it!

Mackenzie could barely talk. "-You gotta' keep wearing them."

"Them what?" Miguel asked, moving on to her neck.

"Condoms Miguel!" Miguel smiled and wrapped his arm around her waist and pulled her down onto his dick. He got up off the bed, while Mackenzie held on to him. Miguel turned around and climbed on top of the bed so that he was now on top. As he laid her back down on the bed slowly, he made sure that they stayed physically connected. Miguel took his time while moving in and out of Mackenzie. With every stroke, he made sure that he paid close attention to her breasts! Mackenzie moaned as he raised her leg in the air and kissed it without skipping a beat!

"Mackenzie."

Mackenzie couldn't keep her eyes open. "Yes?"

Miguel circled his hips and spoke seductively! "I don't want to use them."

Mackenzie could barely think! "What?"

Miguel circled his hips again! "I said I don't want to use them."

"You have to!"

Miguel suddenly pulled out of her, slid down her body, and started licking her pussy! "Oh my God, Miguel! Wait! Oh my God! Stop!"

"What?"

Mackenzie held onto her heart so that it wouldn't jump out of her chest! "What are you doing?"

"You know what I'm doing! What? You don't like it?"

"Miguel?" Miguel ignored her and ate her like he was starving! Mackenzie was at her wit's end! She couldn't talk or think! All that she could do was moan Miguel's name. Miguel stopped and climbed back on top of her!

As soon as he slid inside of her, Miguel knew he only had a couple of minutes! Mackenzie's pussy was drenched! He whispered in her ear. "I'm not using them."

"You have to!" Miguel went deeper but still slow and steady, which made Mackenzie lose it! He started sucking on her neck and breasts while still moving leisurely. "Miguel!"

"Yes!" He answered tirelessly.

"Go faster!"

"No!"

Mackenzie whined! "Why?"

"If I can't get what I want, neither can you." He kissed her and she wrapped her legs around his back.

Mackenzie gnawed on his neck, feeling out of control. "Ok! Ok!"

Miguel slowly increased his speed. "Ok, what?"

Mackenzie was going crazy. "Please!"

"No," he said, slowing down, almost stopping.

Mackenzie was panting, wanting more of him! "Miguel?"

"What?" He asked, kissing the tip of her nose. "What is it, Mackenzie?"

Mackenzie yelled! "Ok, ok!"

Miguel playfully raised his voice, "Ok what?"

Mackenzie raised her head off the bed and stared into his face. "Don't fuckin' play with me!"

Miguel circled his hips, "OK WHAT? ANSWER ME?"

Mackenzie's head dropped back down to the bed, and her eyes instantly closed! She didn't have the strength to say no. "Don't!"

Miguel kissed her lips. "I'm not playing with you, Mackenzie. Answer me!"

He moved faster and deeper inside of Mackenzie, and she loved every bit. "Yes Miguel! Yes!" Miguel pressed on and tried to hang in there until Mackenzie came. He changed his mind and flipped Mackenzie over and started hitting it from behind!

Miguel reached down in front of her and played with her clitoris with his right hand while he pounded away. Mackenzie was now losing her mind! She called out for Miguel to go faster! Miguel took his hand away and put it on the back of her head as he fucked the shit out of her pussy! He was going so fast that she couldn't even moan! All she could do was brace herself on the bed. When he slowed down, he leaned over onto her back and pulled her head up so that he could kiss her. "You ok?"

"Yeah."

"You ready for it?"

"Don't come in me!"

Miguel became agitated with her, telling him what he couldn't do and took it out on her pussy! "What the fuck you say?"

"You can't!"

"I'm coming *all* in your pussy!"

"No!"

"Here it comes!"

"No!" Mackenzie assumed her role and tried to move away. Miguel simultaneously put one hand on her hip, the other on the middle of her back, forcing her ass up in the air.

Miguel laughed triumphantly! "You want me to stop?"

"No!"

"I didn't think so! Ahhhh! Mackenzie! Oh, God!" Miguel yelled out, making sure he gave it all to her! His body started shaking! "FUCK!" After giving her every drop, he rolled off her, onto his back, panting! Mackenzie got up, walked to the bathroom, and closed the door. After she went to the bathroom and washed off, she fixed her hair and rinsed her mouth out.

Miguel walked into the bathroom without knocking and stood behind Mackenzie while they both regarded each other in the mirror. After a few minutes of silence and making funny faces in the mirror, they laughed cathartically! "Miguel, what the hell are we doing? I mean, for real?"

"We are living."

Mackenzie held him and kissed him on his chest. "You're not worried about…"

Miguel kissed her nose and interrupted her. "Are you serious about really giving this a try?"

"Yeah! I just don't want us to bring on more stress to this brand-new thing that we're doing!"

"I hear you and you're right," Miguel said, kissing her. "Why don't you try to get an appointment this week? Until you get on birth control, I'll keep wearing condoms, alright?"

Mackenzie clapped her hands. "See! That's what I'm talking about, baby, communication." Mackenzie kissed his cheek.

Miguel smiled smugly in the mirror while wiping his face with his washcloth. "You know what? I changed my mind! I'm not gonna' wear 'em. I'm sorry!"

Mackenzie's jaw dropped. "Miguel, come on! Stop playing!"

Miguel kissed her and left out of the bathroom.

Mackenzie sat at her desk in her office completing paperwork when her phone rang. She checked the caller ID on her office phone, and it displayed Miguel's name. "Hello!"

"What's up, baby?"

"Nothing much. I'm just finishing up!"

Miguel checked the time on his watch. "What time do you think you'll be at the house?"

"I should be there in about an hour. Why?"

"Just come straight here alright?"

Mackenzie's smile was just as big as day! "Ok! Bye!"

"Bye."

Mackenzie gathered her things together so that she could leave. She reviewed her calendar for the next day and was so excited about going out with Natalie and Bianca on Friday night! They were all going out dancing and she couldn't wait! Miguel had plans to go out with his friends on Friday too, which worked out perfectly! Just then, her cell phone rang. It was Xavier, and she answered. "Hello."

"Hey, stranger. How you doin'?"

"I'm fine. How are you?"

"I'm good! I haven't heard from you in a few days. Everything ok?"

"Oh yeah, everything is fine." Mackenzie said, putting some papers in her file cabinet.

"Do you think you'll have some time to go out this weekend?"

"I don't think so, Xavier! I'm sorry, but I have plans. I'm at work right now and I have to go, I'm sorry!" Xavier was quiet. "Xavier, I'll talk to you later, ok? Bye!" Mackenzie pressed the red phone icon. He called her right back, and Mackenzie answered. "Hello?"

"Mackenzie, what's wrong? Why can't you see me?"

"Xavier, it's too late for you and me! When I was interested, you wanted me and everyone else! It's just too late now, Xavier."

Xavier indignantly sighed. "Come on, Mackenzie, just give me a chance!"

"Xavier please don't make me out to be the bad guy, ok! We tried, and it just didn't work out. I have to go. I'm sorry! Bye!"

Forty-five minutes later, Mackenzie pulled up in Miguel's driveway. After she placed the gear in park, she took a deep breath and turned her truck off. Mackenzie glanced at how Miguel's car was gleaming in the sunshine! She felt the same on the inside! Miguel was taking her breath away! Ever since their agreement, he did something special for her every day. Monday, he took her to dinner and to see a play downtown. Tuesday, he cooked dinner at his house and gave her a full body massage. Wednesday, he surprised her at her job with flowers and lunch, but today *she* had something for him! Mackenzie rang the bell and Miguel greeted her at the door with a kiss. "Hey baby!"

"Hey!"

Miguel led her inside. "How was work?"

"Work was cool! What did you do today?"

Miguel embraced Mackenzie and kissed her on the nose. "I took care of some business, ran some errands, chilled out, you know, vacation stuff!"

"When do you go back to work?"

Miguel kissed her cheek! "Monday!"

Mackenzie playfully jabbed him in the stomach! "Saturday is the day after tomorrow, Miguellllll!"

"I know Mackenzie! It usually is!"

Mackenzie hit him with the pillow on the sofa. "Are you reconsidering?"

"Nah, I don't think so! What about you?"

"I think I'm good too!" Mackenzie said, placing the pillow back on the couch.

"Mackenzie, are you sure about this?"

Mackenzie shook her head and pointed her finger at him! "Ummmm, are *you* sure?"

Miguel confidently looked at her. "Yeah, I'm sure!"

"Well alright then, I'm sure too!" Both of them laughed out loud.

Mackenzie kissed him on the cheek. "So, who's going out with you tomorrow?"

"Let me see! It's going to be about six of us riding tomorrow. It's gonna' be me, Teo, Trini, Brad, Chris, Xavier, and Nate, so that's seven! We're riding out from here."

Mackenzie took a seat on the couch and just sat there in disbelief. "Miguel, did you say Xavier?"

"Yeah! Why?"

Mackenzie placed the back of her hand on her forehead and sighed. "Because that might be the man I was dating."

Miguel nonchalantly shrugged his shoulders. "I just met him not too long ago through my boy Chris. He just bought a bike and wanted to ride with us. I guess I'll see when he comes over, huh?"

Mackenzie shook her head and covered her face. "I'm just gonna get ready at my house tomorrow."

"Why? I mean, it was nothing, right?"

Mackenzie stood up and paced the floor a bit. "Right, but I don't think he's getting the point."

"What do you mean by that? What's going on?"

Mackenzie heard the anger brewing in Miguel's voice. She got anxious and thought twice about saying anything else.

"Mackenzie, if something is going on, you need to tell me now."

Mackenzie took a deep breath and explained, "Miguel, Xavier is the same guy who was texting me that day when I punched your friend in the face. He called me today, wanting to know if he could see me on Saturday. I told him no and that it was too late for us. Then I told him I had to go."

Miguel scrutinized her face. "That's it?"

Mackenzie raised her right hand. "Yes, your honor, that's it!" Mackenzie sat down on the couch and let her head fall back onto the cushion.

Miguel sat down next to her. "He didn't kiss you like this?"

Miguel kissed Mackenzie and smiled. Mackenzie laughed, "No, he didn't!"

"You sure y'all didn't have relations?" Mackenzie cracked up laughing, got up, and started walking toward the stairs. "Where are you going?"

Mackenzie laughed, "I'm going to the bathroom, if you don't mind!"

"Come here for a minute!" Mackenzie walked back over to the couch and sat back down next to him. "Mackenzie, I know we're both going out tomorrow night with our friends so, I thought maybe we could do something special tonight."

Mackenzie nodded her head and smiled. "Of course. What did you have in mind?"

Miguel handed Mackenzie a rectangular jewelry box. "First, I want to give you this." Mackenzie just looked at him. "Open it!"

Mackenzie's fingers were fidgety while opening the box! Once opened, her mouth hit the floor! "Miguel! Oh my God! It's beautiful!" He bought her a gold necklace with a gold heart-shaped Spinner Locket!

Miguel took it out of the box. "This is how you open it!" He opened the locket and held it in front of her. "Read what's inside!" Mackenzie inspected the inscription:

I met you!

I liked you!

We're friends!

I AM IN LOVE WITH YOU!

Just like that and all in one week!

Mackenzie stared at Miguel. She was about to ask him a question, but Miguel read her loud and clear. He kissed her lips and then the tip of her nose. "Before you even say anything, yes, I'm serious and yes, I mean it! I didn't think it was going to happen this fast."

She kissed him while he opened her blouse. He stopped undressing Mackenzie! "You didn't have this on this morning!" Mackenzie just stared at him and bit her bottom lip. Mackenzie had on a light pink and gray lace push-up bra underneath a light pink camisole. He dragged her skirt off, exposing her gray thigh-high stockings and her pink and gray laced low-rise hipsters. Mackenzie stood up and walked over to the door. "Where are you going?"

"I have something for you!"

"I already see it!"

Mackenzie put her hands on her hips! "Be quiet!" She purposefully bent over from the waist to search in her bag.

Miguel couldn't take her teasing him anymore! "Mackenzie, you need to stop playing and come on over here!"

Mackenzie stood up and walked over to him with something behind her back. "I have a little something for you too!" Mackenzie handed him a card. Miguel took the envelope and opened it while

Mackenzie sat down next to him. There was an *M* printed in gold on the front of the cream-colored card. When he opened it, Mackenzie sat back.

Miguel, where do I begin!? I am so happy right now that I don't know where to start!

In this week alone, you have completely uplifted me!

You listen to me. You talk to me, and you sincerely care.

Miguel, if this doesn't work out,

I wouldn't regret a single moment that I have shared with you!

I will always be there for you because

I am utterly in love with you!

Mackenzie

Miguel closed the card and just held it in his hand for a moment, thinking of what she wrote. He put the card down on the table, took the locket he bought for her and put it around her neck. Miguel then took her hand and led her upstairs to his bedroom. He had candles lit all around the bedroom and bathroom.

Mackenzie pulled his shirt off and kissed his chest. "I let my job know I would be in a little late tomorrow."

"I don't think you're going to make it in at all!"

"Miguel, you know we should wear them until I at least get a period."

He chuckled while sucking on her neck. "If that is what you want."

"Alright!" He finished where he left off and pushed her onto the bed.

He laid his body on top of hers. "So, you're in love with me?"

"Yes! I am in love with you, Miguel. Are you in love with me?" Miguel didn't reply. He was too busy playing with her breasts. Mackenzie sat up. "I am in love with you, Miguel."

He kissed her. "And I'm in love with you!" They made love until morning! Mackenzie only worked a half-day!

Mackenzie was at her house, getting ready to go to the club with Natalie and Bianca. She had on a Rachel Roy Alex Silk Jersey Dress. It was a burgundy/rust color and resembled a sexy ass toga! Mackenzie was about to leave out the house when she remembered that the purse she wanted to wear was over at Miguel's house. She called Miguel! "Hello?"

"Hey baby, what's going on?"

"I left one of my pocketbooks over at your house. Can I come and get it real quick before y'all leave?"

Miguel glanced at his watch. "Yeah, when are you coming?"

"I should be there in about thirty minutes. Is that ok?"

"Yeah! I'll be here!"

"Alright, bye!" Thirty minutes later, Mackenzie arrived at the corner of Miguel's block. She called Natalie after pulling up in his driveway! "Hey Natalie! I'll be there in about twenty-five minutes."

Natalie snapped her fingers. "Yessssss! Alright! We are here!"

Mackenzie snapped her fingers out loud! "-And I'm coming!"

"Alright girl, be careful!"

"I will!" Mackenzie ended the call, put her phone in her purse, and turned the truck off. There were bikes in the yard and parked in the street in front of the house! Mackenzie's heart started beating, thinking about if Xavier was inside Miguel's house! "Fuck it!" Mackenzie grabbed her purse, walked up to the opened doorway, rang the bell, and proceeded inside. "Hello? Miguel?"

Miguel shuffled to the door! "Hey baby!" He gave her a big ole' slobbery-beer kiss and Mackenzie laughed. "You look so sexy!" He reached in closer to her ear while placing a wet one on her neck. "I got something for you upstairs!"

Mackenzie giggled and pushed him away! "You've been drinking, huh?"

"Just a couple of beers!"

"Miguel, please be careful driving. Promise me you'll be careful!"

"I promise!" He kissed her and held her body tight!

"Let me get my bag and get out of here!"

Miguel raised his eyebrows as if he recalled something important. "Wait, let me introduce you before you go upstairs!"

Mackenzie grabbed his arm and made him stop. "Miguel, is the guy named Xavier here?"

"Yeah, he's here! Come on!" Miguel held her hand and walked with her to the living room. The guys were standing and sitting around drinking beer and listening to music. Miguel held her tight and introduced her to the guys. "Guys, this is my woman, Mackenzie! Mackenzie, these are the guys!"

"Hi, Mackenzie!" They all said in unison, except Xavier!

Mackenzie waved her trembling hand at the guys! "Hi, guys!"

Teo raised his beer in the air. "What's up, Mackenzie?"

"Hey, Teo!"

Teo's eyes turned cold as he walked over to where they were standing. "Where are you going dressed like that? Miguel, you lettin' her out looking like that?" Mackenzie gave him a mean look, then quickly smiled. Teo laughed! "I'm just playin' Mackenzie!"

Mackenzie's laughter quickly came to a halt when Xavier walked over toward the three of them. He was mad! Mackenzie just hoped that Xavier wouldn't act a fool! "Miguel, can I talk to you for a minute in the kitchen?" Xavier asked, not even acknowledging Mackenzie.

"Sure." Mackenzie didn't say a word. Teo, Xavier, and Miguel walked toward the kitchen. Mackenzie walked up the living room stairs to get her purse from the loft on the third floor. She couldn't believe that Xavier was at Miguel's house! Mackenzie grabbed her phone from inside of her purse and called Natalie!

~

Miguel and Xavier strode into the kitchen while Teo stood nearby in the doorway between the kitchen and the dining room. Xavier and Miguel sat down at the kitchen table across from one another. Miguel studied Xavier's behavior, waiting to hear what he had to say. "What's up, Xavier?"

Xavier sat back in the chair, looked down at the table, and then at Teo. "Miguel, I don't mean no disrespect, but Mackenzie and I are together."

Miguel could tell that he was lying and just stared at Xavier. "And how is that?" Miguel inquired, as if he was truly surprised.

Xavier aimed to tell his version of events. "We just had a big argument the other day, but we've been together for like two months!"

Miguel stared at him with so much intensity that it made Xavier uncomfortable. "You know what? I just met her the other day! I think it was Wednesday! When was the last time y'all been together?"

"Tuesday night."

Teo closed his eyes and just shook his head. He knew the deal and how Miguel had Mackenzie on lock all week! Miguel folded his hands on the table and stared at Xavier! "Xavier, it's over between you and Mackenzie, and seriously, I think you should probably leave."

Xavier was stuck-on-stupid! "Alright just go get Mackenzie and tell her…"

Miguel tilted his head to the side while still keeping his hands interlocked on the table. "Pussy, I ain't doin' shit! Now what you think you had with Mackenzie is over! **IT'S DONE**! Accept it and move the fuck on because she belongs to me!" Even though Xavier didn't know Miguel that well, he knew about his reputation, so he didn't push the issue. Xavier got up, pushed his chair in, and left out of the house through the kitchen door.

Miguel sat there for a minute listening to Xavier's bike roll out and thought of how much he loved Mackenzie. He didn't even want to talk to any of his old joins'! It was time to settle down! Mackenzie was going to be the one!

Teo chuckled and slapped on the doorframe! "That was some funny-ass shit! Lil'-man was lying from the gate!"

Miguel mocked Xavier! *"Just go get Mackenzie!* What the fuck?" Both laughed their asses off!

Mackenzie heard Miguel laughing from the second-floor hallway and came down the kitchen stairs. "Miguel, I'm leaving! I searched all around on the third floor and I couldn't find it and I'm late!" Miguel and Teo turned to Mackenzie. "Why are y'all looking at me like that? Do I have a boogie in my nose or something?!"

Miguel and Teo laughed! Miguel kissed Mackenzie's hand! "Baby, have a good time and be careful, ok?"

"You be careful too! I'm serious! Please be careful!" She kissed him on the forehead and hugged him. Mackenzie pointed to Teo! "You better be careful too!"

Teo threw up the peace sign! "Alright!"

~2:47 am ~

Mackenzie, Natalie, and Bianca were having a ball dancing their asses off on the dance floor! Mackenzie went to the bathroom to check her hair and to see if Miguel had called her. She inspected her hair and checked her phone. Her heart was pounding so hard!

Mackenzie had missed him so much! She didn't call Miguel because she didn't want to smother him. Mackenzie smiled at the display showing two text messages and opened one of them. The first message was from Xavier.

I guess that's it, huh? You could have told me you were seeing someone! I know you are a good woman, so I'm going to say this to you. Miguel has a reputation for being a true player...

Mackenzie took a deep breath and deleted the message. The second message was from Miguel about five minutes ago.

I don't mean to interrupt, but I need you!

Mackenzie laughed and shimmied her shoulders while composing her reply.

~

Miguel was at the pool hall with Teo and some others when his phone vibrated. It was a text from Mackenzie.

I'm sorry! I didn't get that! Did you say that you missed me? Or did you say that you need to get some of this pussy?

Miguel laughed and shook his head! He text her back, while Teo went to the bathroom.

~

Mackenzie was at the bar, ordering a sprite while watching Natalie and Bianca dance. The bartender handed her the sprite as she felt her phone vibrate. It was Miguel.

Go home.

Pack a bag for about 2 days.

Then, call me when you're ready.

Mackenzie sashayed and drank the rest of her Sprite! She danced her way over to Natalie and Bianca, letting them know she was leaving.

Natalie reached over to Mackenzie's ear. "Call me when you get home, since I'm dropping Bianca off!"

"Ok, I will!" Mackenzie hugged Natalie and then gave one to Bianca.

Bianca was drunk as hell. "Be careful driving home!"

Mackenzie gave them a girly salute. "Yes ma'am! Y'all be careful!"

~3:52 a.m. ~

After Mackenzie sent Natalie a text that she was safely at home, she showered, packed some clothes, and then called Miguel. He picked up on the first ring. "Hey baby! You ready?"

"Yes!"

"I'm outside waiting."

"Ok, I'll be right out!" She had on a pair of sandals, shorts, and an off-the-shoulder tee shirt with no bra. Mackenzie grabbed her purse, sprayed on some perfume, grabbed her bag, and went to the door.

When she opened the door, Miguel was standing right there. He walked in the door and kissed her! Mackenzie dropped her things on the floor and held her man in her arms. Miguel closed the door as he walked through, still kissing Mackenzie. She pulled on his pants, trying to unbuckle them while Miguel unbuttoned and pulled down her shorts. Miguel picked her up and took her upstairs while still kissing her.

After he arrived at the top of the stairs, he pulled his lips away and smiled. "Which way?" Mackenzie pointed to her room and Miguel walked right in. He laid her on the bed and pulled her thong down. Miguel then ate her out, thoroughly. She had to beg him to stop! He pulled down his pants and climbed on top of her! "You have a lovely house, baby!"

"Thank you!"

"Not for long, though!"

"What?"

"You heard me!" He said, shoving his dick inside of her. "Mackenzie, I missed you!"

"I missed you too!" Miguel kissed her neck while she held him close. As he made love to Mackenzie, she turned her head away from him. Her eyes filled with tears.

Miguel saw them and slowed down. "Mackenzie." Mackenzie turned her head and let him see her face. She could not hold the tears back any longer. Miguel wiped the tears from her face and kissed her eyes while steadily moving inside of her. Mackenzie wrapped her legs around his back and held on to him tight. He fixated on Mackenzie's eyes the whole time he moved inside of her. Miguel lowered his upper body onto her chest. "Mackenzie," he said, speeding up a bit, "I can't hold it any longer!"

"Ok!"

"I'm coming inside of you!"

"Ok!" Mackenzie kissed him and held on to the back of his head, trying to stifle his groaning. He pulled away, letting the neighbors know he was in the house while coming inside of her. Miguel kissed her again while holding on to her tight. They fell asleep immediately afterward with Mackenzie's head on Miguel's chest.

Miguel woke up first and watched her breathing. She was by far the most honest, prettiest, and sexiest woman he had ever been with. He got out of bed, entered her bathroom, took a quick shower, and used her toothbrush to brush his teeth! Miguel walked back into Mackenzie's bedroom and put his clothes on. Mackenzie woke up.

"Right, this *is* Saturday morning! The end of the pact! So, you're leaving out, huh?"

"I need you to get up and get dressed! I have a surprise for you!" Mackenzie jumped up and paraded to the bathroom to get herself ready. It only took her about twenty minutes to get showered, dressed, and ready to go. Mackenzie walked down the stairs and saw that he had already taken her bag to the car. She picked up her purse and keys from the couch and headed out of the door.

As Mackenzie walked toward the car, she could see Miguel sitting in the car talking on the phone. When she walked closer to the car, he ended the call. She opened the passenger side door and sat down inside. He kissed her on the cheek. "Miguel, where are we going?"

"Florida."

Mackenzie gasped! "What? For how long?"

"How long do you want to stay?"

"Miguel, I'm not playing! How long?"

"Can you stay for three days?"

Mackenzie rummaged through her purse for her phone. "I have to talk to my boss first."

"Mackenzie, tell them you had an emergency, and you had to go out of town."

"Are you trying to get me fired? I need to be back by Monday!"

Miguel gave her another kiss before he pulled off to the airport. "I think I like you!"

Chapter 5 – Oceans of Love

When they arrived in Florida, at the Fort Lauderdale-Hollywood International Airport, they stayed at the St. Regis Bal Harbour Luxury Resort. The hotel was right on the beach! It reminded Mackenzie of the old television show Fantasy Island! She did her share of traveling, but St. Regis had to be one of the most serene places she had ever visited.

The front desk clerk handed Miguel his room card keys. "Thank you, Mr. Conway. Please let us know if there is anything that we can do to make your stay more enjoyable!"

"Thank you." Miguel took the keys and held Mackenzie's hand as they walked across the marble floors toward the elevators to the tenth floor. Mackenzie couldn't believe she was in Florida with Miguel! She felt her phone vibrating in her purse. Mackenzie opened her purse and pulled out her phone to see who it was. She quickly put the phone back in her purse.

"Everything ok?"

"Yes."

"What's up?"

"Nothing, I'm ok!" Mackenzie gave him a quaint smile.

Miguel felt his anger intensifying by the second! "Who was that?"

Mackenzie tilted her head to the side. "Why are you asking me that?"

"Because you're obviously feeling some kind of way about whoever called you!"

Mackenzie took a deep breath. "It was Xavier."

Miguel was furious. "What?"

"Miguel, please don't be upset." Mackenzie was very calm and to the point while speaking to him. "He sent me a text the other day, and he just called. I haven't talked to him, and I haven't seen him since your house." The elevator doors opened, and they walked through.

Miguel turned to her in the hallway. "Mackenzie, I'm not upset with you." He lovingly kissed her lips, "Don't you worry about a thing, ok? We are here to have fun and to enjoy ourselves!" Mackenzie smiled and hugged him. They walked down the hall to their room. Miguel opened the door, and the suite just took Mackenzie's breath away! The living room had lovely modern furniture with a view overlooking the ocean. There was a huge plasma TV suspended on the wall with beautiful fresh flowers placed all around the room! The suite was incredible!

"Do you like it?" Miguel asked, putting the card keys on the living room table.

"What? Miguel this suite is absolutely beautiful! Oh, my goodness!" She ran into the master bedroom. "It's amazing Miguel!"

Miguel laughed, opening the door for the attendant with their bags. He handed the attendant a tip and shook his hand. "Thanks, man."

"You're welcome, sir!"

Mackenzie opened the balcony doors and just could not believe the view from where she was standing! Miguel came up behind her. "Miguel, thank you for bringing me here with you!"

"Thank you for coming with me!" Miguel kissed her passionately. He took off his shirt and slowly removed her blouse, revealing her bra.

She immediately turned around, so that she was facing him! "Oh, so you're going to let everyone see me topless?"

"You're not topless." He reached around, unhooked her bra, allowed it to fall on the balcony floor, and then pulled her in close. "Now you're topless!" Miguel kissed her lips, picked her up, and took her over to the bed.

"Miguel, what about the balcony?"

Miguel pulled her pants off and pulled her panties down when she grabbed his hands. "I wanted to take a shower first!"

"I can't wait until then." He yanked her panties off and pulled down his pants. "Get on all fours!" Mackenzie smiled a little and shook her head no. "What?"

She moved in close so that they were nose to nose. "You heard me! I said no! What? You can't fuckin' hear!" Miguel laughed and pulled her legs to the edge of the bed. Mackenzie kindly pulled them back onto the bed. Miguel's dick was throbbing hard! He crawled on top of her and started devouring her pussy. Her faint moaning quickly transformed into squeals and shrieks of ecstasy! Mackenzie pushed Miguel's head up and practically tackled him over on his back.

"It's my turn!" Mackenzie was going to ride him, but she changed her position!

Miguel was about to have a heart attack! "Mackenzie!" She put his dick in her hand and began to slowly taste him with her tongue as if she was licking a huge taffy. Miguel started breathing heavily, and she hadn't even put him in her mouth yet. Mackenzie was ready to eat, so she gobbled him up! Miguel cursed at her while he watched her suck his dick. After about ten minutes, he couldn't take it anymore! It was too much for him to handle, so he pulled her head up and jumped off the bed. "Turn around!"

"I said no!" His dick was so damn hard that he thought it was going to fucking explode if he didn't get inside of her soon.

"Mackenzie, can you turn around, baby? I need you!"

"I will if you let me suck it some more!" Miguel rolled on his back and Mackenzie went to work. Mackenzie sucked his dick as if it was the last thing she was *ever* going to taste! Miguel loved the way she was sucking his dick, but he didn't want to come just yet! He lifted her head and turned her on all fours.

He swiftly put his dick inside of her. Miguel was motionless as he kissed all over her back. "Why did you tell me no, Mackenzie?"

Mackenzie sucked her teeth. "What difference does it make?"

Miguel took a couple of breaths and started moving slowly! "Did I ever tell you no, Mackenzie?"

"No." Miguel increased his stride more and more! He was pounding her pussy hard as ever! Mackenzie was so loud that Miguel thought that maybe he should have closed the balcony doors! "Oh my God! Please forgive me!" Miguel slowed down! He didn't want the neighbors to think he was hurting her, even though Mackenzie was asking for more. He pulled out and turned her on her back.

"Are you going to be good?"

"Yes, I'm going to be good!" He sucked on her breasts and neck. "Miguel, I need you inside! Please!" Miguel smiled and slid his dick right back inside of her! She wrapped her legs around him and kissed him. "Baby, you can't keep coming inside of me!"

"Stop telling me what I can't do!"

"I'm serious Miguel!"

He stopped moving and stared into her eyes without blinking. "If you don't want to be with me, tell me now." Mackenzie stared at him because his voice sounded like he was more than upset. Miguel sounded as if he was wounded.

Mackenzie caressed his face with her hands. "I want to be with you! It's just that…"

"It's just what?" Miguel roared while creating distance between them.

Mackenzie pulled him back on top of her. "I want to be with you, Miguel. I'm just unsure about whether you and I are ready for that right now."

"Mackenzie, I'm a grown-ass fuckin' man! I know when I'm ready for something, especially when I say that I am! I'm ready for whatever! -Especially kids! I love kids and you know that! I'm more than ready to have one if it happens. The question is, are you?"

Mackenzie closed her eyes and shook her head. "So, is that it? If it happens, it happens?"

He kissed her lips and whispered in her ear, "It will happen."

"But not right now, right?" Mackenzie tried her hardest to suppress her apprehension.

Miguel put her leg up in the air and then let it back down over his shoulder. "Mackenzie." He moved deeper inside of her, knowing how much she loved it when he did that. Mackenzie called on the Lord! "Mackenzie?"

Mackenzie's eyes were closed. "Yes"

"Mackenzie, look at me!" Mackenzie opened her eyes and smiled at him. She took her hands, caressed his face, and kissed him. "Mackenzie, I love you."

Her smile went away. "What did you say to me?"

"I love you."

Mackenzie was astounded. "Don't tell me you love me because you love my pussy!" Miguel stopped and laughed so hard that Mackenzie had to laugh with him! "I'm serious Miguel!" Miguel made love to her while kissing and sucking on her neck and breasts. He moved faster this time and knew that Mackenzie was close to climaxing. Miguel held on to her real tight, but Mackenzie couldn't take it anymore. "Oh my God! Miguel!"

"Yes!" Mackenzie was making all kinds of noises and all of them turned him on! "Put your legs up!" He put her legs on his shoulders and leaned all the way forward on top of her.

"Oh, Miguel! Oh, God!"

"Do you love me, Mackenzie?"

"Yes, I do! Oh God, I do! I love you, Miguel! I love you! Give it to me please!" Mackenzie's insides shook, and Miguel came deep inside of her.

His ejaculate shot out like a rocket. "Mackenzie, your pussy is so fucking good! Goddamn!" Miguel pulled out of her and collapsed onto the bed beside her while panting. After catching his breath, he rolled on his side, facing her. Mackenzie kissed his lips and smiled. Miguel kissed her neck. "Is it all mine, baby?"

"If you want it to be!"

"Yes, I want it to be! It has to be!"

Mackenzie ran her fingers through the hair on his chest! "We'll see!"

~

After a couple of hours, Miguel took Mackenzie shopping at the boutiques by Collins Ave for some clothes, shoes, and a bathing suit. As Mackenzie modeled for Miguel at Saks Fifth Avenue, he thought about how beautiful she was and how much he loved being around her. He loved how she could make him laugh at the drop of a dime! "Miguel, can you come here, please?" Miguel stood up from his chair and went to her dressing booth. When he opened the door, Mackenzie was standing with her back to him. "Can you unzip me?" Miguel unzipped her dress and kissed her back. Mackenzie turned around and kissed him. "Thank you!" Miguel smiled and just stood there.

While keeping her head still, her eyes moved to his crotch and then back up to his eyes while licking her lips. Miguel laughed as she kissed him and unbuckled his pants. He pulled away, "No."

It was too late because Mackenzie had already whipped his strength out! "I just want a taste!"

Miguel shook his head. "Alright, just a little bit!" Mackenzie smiled and went to work. Miguel's body quivered with excitement! People were talking in the other rooms, and he was trying to keep an ear out for the store's employees. He watched her in the full-length mirror in front of him and was blown away at the sight of her sucking his dick. Her dress fell to the floor showing her ass decorated with her red thong! "Baby stop!" Mackenzie kept going and started licking his balls. Miguel moaned more and closed his eyes. She returned to his dick and Miguel could not take it anymore. He had to fuck her right there and then because he wasn't walking out of that store with a rock-hard dick!

He opened his eyes and made sure the door was locked. Miguel turned his head and found a chair. He pulled her head from his dick. "Get up!" Mackenzie did as she was told as Miguel positioned her in front of the chair. "Turn around and bend over!" As Mackenzie turned around and bent over, Miguel grabbed her thong and tore it apart! He put one hand on her hip and put his dick inside with the other.

They were both quiet until Mackenzie couldn't hold it anymore. She started moaning and calling his name. Miguel was so turned on! He knew others could hear Mackenzie calling his name! Feeling her ass smacking from his dick slamming into her wet pussy echoed in the dressing room! "Where you want it?" Miguel said, trying to whisper.

"On my ass!"

"No!"

"On my back!"

"No! Here it comes! Where?"

"In my mouth!"

"Turn around! Turn around!" Miguel pulled out. Mackenzie turned around and quickly dropped to her knees, grabbed his penis, and put it in her mouth! Miguel couldn't help but squeal as he watched her sucking all the come out of his dick! "Damn Mackenzie! Are you trying to kill me?"

She licked her lips. "No!"

Miguel realized she had swallowed it. "Was it a lot?"

"Yeah! It was sweet too!" Mackenzie raised her eyebrow and laughed!

Miguel took a deep breath and pulled her up off the floor and kissed her neck. "I love you, Mackenzie!"

~

After bringing their things back to the room, they showered together, dressed, and ate dinner at the hotel. Mackenzie had an idea and shared it with Miguel as they left the restaurant. They walked up to their suite, grabbed a blanket, and took it to the beach so that they could enjoy the night. Mackenzie laid in his lap and stared out at the water while Miguel did the same. Mackenzie inhaled the fresh ocean air. "This moment right here is the moment that I will always remember." She moved in closer to him and Miguel kissed her on the top of her head. "Miguel, why are we here?"

Miguel watched the water while trying to redirect her thoughts. "I'm here because I have to take care of some business and I wanted you to come with me." Mackenzie smiled. "It won't take long, though. -A couple of hours tomorrow morning."

"We never really talked about exactly what you do. I mean, I know you told me you were an independent consultant, but what do you consult with your clients?"

Miguel ended her inquiry. "Mackenzie, I want us to relax and enjoy ourselves as much as we can. When we get back to Philly, I will explain everything that you want to know about the work that I do, ok?" He said assuredly while playing in her hair. Mackenzie shook her head yes and turned over so that she could lie on the blanket. Miguel laid down beside her and contemplated her initial question.

"Miguel, what happened to the last woman you were in love with?"

"I wasn't in love, but I thought I was. She told me she was pregnant, and I told her I was in love with her. It filled me with all kinds of emotions when she told me." His face turned bitter, "… and then she said that she didn't want the baby. To make a long story short, she just wanted some money!"

Mackenzie was furious! She sat up and turned toward him so that she could get the full story. He gave her tidbits here and there, but she wanted to know the complete story! "Why the hell did she do that?"

"She knew I had money, and she wanted it!"

"What happened? Did she have an abortion?" The ocean's movement demanded Miguel's attention. He felt as if he was drifting out! Miguel turned his head to Mackenzie and smiled. He completely ignored her questions and said what *he* wanted to say about the situation.

"She died."

"What happened?"

Miguel allowed the ocean to hypnotize him with its infinite movement. "Her house caught on fire."

Mackenzie still didn't get a full understanding of what happened, but she knew he was deeply affected by it. He had a bleak expression on his face the whole time he spoke. Mackenzie tapped Miguel's arm, and he looked up at her. She put up her index finger and told him to come here. Mackenzie kissed him. "I would never do that to you. Even if things didn't work out between us, I would never hurt you like that! Never!"

Miguel smiled! "Let's make another deal! If we make it to…."

"Miguel, I don't think that we should make any more deals." Mackenzie replied, feeling overwhelmed by adding more stipulations to their arrangement.

Miguel tried to get her to listen! "No, hear me out! Hear me out! It's July now. If we stay together for one year and you're not pregnant, let's get married and start our family!"

Mackenzie was scared shitless! Her fear turned right into deflection! "You are so full of shit! How are you going to suggest that we get married next year if we're still together? What if you meet someone next month and change your mind? Or what if you meet someone? You fuck her! The condom breaks with her, and she gets pregnant! Miguel, I love you, but I don't know what's going to happen between now and next year and neither do you."

Miguel tried not to get upset! "I know we can make this into whatever we want it to be, Mackenzie! I want to make you happy and I'm making you happy! I want to love you and that's what I'm doing! Mackenzie, I am your man because I want to be! I know I can meet any woman and fuck her! I'm concentrating on you and me just like you are! Don't try to make my feelings out to be any less than yours!"

"Miguel, I'm not trying to say that!"

"Well, what *are* you saying? Do you believe me when I say the things that I say to you?"

"Yes!"

Miguel became enraged. "Well, why do you always say shit like *what if you change your mind*, or *what if you meet someone else,* or *what if you fuck someone else?* You gotta stop that shit!"

Mackenzie stayed calm. "I'm just trying to be fair and understand how you might feel later on! You are the one that said that you weren't trying to get serious Miguel!"

"Yeah, I did! Then I said, ok, I do want to get serious with you! It's not like, every day I'm saying some different shit! Mackenzie, it's difficult enough telling you how I feel! Stop adding in all that *'you might do this'* bullshit! You should take what I'm saying for what it is if, or until, I give you an actual reason to doubt me!"

Mackenzie felt horrible because she knew he was right. She took a deep breath. "I'm sorry. You're right." Mackenzie stood up, took a couple of steps away from the blanket, and walked closer to the water. She was in unfamiliar territory with how she felt about

Miguel. Mackenzie couldn't help but feel like she was putting herself at risk for the biggest heartbreak of her life! She felt extremely vulnerable and started tearing up. Miguel stood up and walked over to her. Mackenzie heard him and tried to clean up her face so that he wouldn't see her crying.

"Don't cry." Miguel kissed her lips and eyes. "We're both new at this!"

"And how do you know I've never been in love before?"

"Were you?"

Mackenzie shook her head no. She thought about her ex-boyfriend Darien, who died six months ago. Mackenzie remembered how they used to have so much fun while viewing the water. "We, Darien, and I, talked about marriage and having a family but not as if *he and I* were going to have them together! I loved him more as a friend than anything else." Mackenzie could not focus her eyes on anything except the ocean's unwavering movement.

Miguel stood in front of her so that she could only see him. He caressed her face and kissed Mackenzie's lips. Miguel wrapped his arms around Mackenzie and kissed her neck. "In a year, we are getting married, and we are gonna start a family. Are you good with that?"

Mackenzie raised her head to the heavens in trepidation. "Yes, but one thing!"

Miguel's face turned dry. He removed his hands from around her. "What is it now? You want to ask me if, I'm sure?" He asked angrily!

"No! Why are you talking to me like that? You don't even know what I was going to say! You know what? You need to watch yourself and how you talk to me sometimes!"

Miguel kicked the sand and shook his head in shame. "You're right. I'm sorry!" Mackenzie just stood there and explored the beach with her eyes for a minute or two. Miguel broke the silence after a few minutes. "I apologize. What were you going to say?" Mackenzie just shook her head as if she didn't want to talk. "I'm sorry about coming at you like that. Talk to me. Please!"

Mackenzie closed her eyes and resumed her gaze out in the distance.

"What is it?"

Mackenzie started crying again. "I'm scared! All of this just seems too good to be true! I am afraid that we're moving too fast!"

Miguel held her in his arms. "It's real. I know it usually doesn't happen like this, but it is real!"

Mackenzie closed her eyes and pinched the bridge of her nose, trying to fight through her distress. "What if I get pregnant before next year, Miguel?"

"If you get pregnant before next year, then we will just get married before the baby comes!"

"Miguel, I love you! I would not want you to marry me because I'm having your baby!"

Miguel kissed her nose. "I understand! Let's just agree that what we said will pop off next year then, all right? And if you get pregnant before then, we'll figure it out."

"Alright, batman!" Mackenzie pushed Miguel and tried to run away. Miguel caught up with her in no time at all. He picked her up, ran back to the blanket, and laid her down. She laughed so hard she could barely catch her breath!

Miguel smiled at her while she tried to catch her breath. "Mackenzie, after knowing someone for a week, going to the movies or dinner is about as far as I would take them! I know this is going fast, but I'm not doing it! That's just the way it's going!" Mackenzie wholeheartedly understood! It was as if they were at love's mercy.

"It's so beautiful out here." Mackenzie laid her head on his chest. She felt her phone vibrating and went to get it.

Miguel grabbed her hands and kissed them. "Don't answer that, baby! Come here and let's watch the sun go down and let's be all romantical and shit!!!" Mackenzie and Miguel cracked up laughing! "Tomorrow morning, I'm going to meet up with a couple of friends of mine. Like I said, I will only be gone for about three or four hours."

"Alright, while you're doing that, I'll probably visit a friend of mine!"

"Let's get something sweet to eat!"

~9:36 am ~

Mackenzie woke up alone in bed. There was a white rose on his pillow with a note on the small dresser next to the bed:

Mackenzie, I left your key card in the top drawer. I'll call you later on, to see how you're doing. I left you some money in the drawer in case you wanted to get something while you were out.

I love you!

Mackenzie opened the dresser drawer. He placed the key card on top of the money. Mackenzie counted three thousand dollars. She laughed, putting the money back in the drawer. Mackenzie got up, hopped in the shower, and called her friend Tommy. She was so excited about spending some time with him. He immediately picked up the phone and Mackenzie couldn't hold back. "Hey, Tommy!"

"Hey, girl! What the hell are you doing in Florida?"

"I'm here with my man!"

Tommy playfully coughed! "Your man?! And what is this man's name?"

"Tommy, stop playing! Girl, you know it's Miguel!"

"Oh yeah! Miguel the Beast! Oooooh, girl! I can't wait to meet!"

Mackenzie cracked up laughing. "What are you doing today?"

Tommy cleared his throat as if he was about to make an announcement! "Well, after breakfast, I'm supposed to do a little shopping, compliments of my dear and loving *sponsor,* Mr. Starks!" Mr. Starks was a name that Tommy used for his long-time wealthy beau, whose real name Tommy would never tell.

Mackenzie laid on the bed and talked to Tommy just like they did when they were in college. "Mr. Starks is still on the scene, huh?"

"Very much so, honey! So, I am gonna shop 'til I drop, and then tonight is just a blur baby! A complete blurrr!"

"Why don't we go shopping?"

Tommy laughed! "Ok! I'll come and pick you up around twelve. Where are you staying?"

"We're at St. Regis in Bal Harbour!"

Tommy cleared his throat again. "Oh, Mr. Beast is healthy, huh?"

"Girl stop! I'll meet you out front at twelve!"

"Ok, sweetie! Bye!"

Mackenzie and Tommy were roommates from college and were very close. In college, Tommy would always use Mackenzie's make-up and toiletries when he first 'came out' and Mackenzie couldn't stand it! So, to keep him from always using her shit, they shopped together. By junior year, *he* would take *her* shopping with *him*! She loved him like the brother/sister she never had. When he moved to Florida, they made a promise to talk to each other at least once a week.

~12:10 pm ~

While Mackenzie waited for Tommy to pick her up, she sat outside the hotel and called Miguel.

Miguel's phone vibrated. He picked up his phone and viewed her contact photo, which he took while she was asleep. Miguel answered it immediately. "Hey baby."

"Hey! How's it going?"

"Everything's good! What are you doing?"

Mackenzie checked around to see if Tommy was about to pull up. "I'm about to go out!"

"Ok, I should be back around three."

"Alright, be safe, ok?"

"Don't worry, I will."

The bellman walked up to Mackenzie. "Excuse me, Ms. The gentleman over there is waiting for you."

"Ok, thank you." Mackenzie said, hoping that Miguel didn't hear the doorman's announcement. "Miguel, I'll see you later!"

"Mackenzie?" Miguel's tone completely changed when he overheard what the bellman said. "Who are you going out with?"

"A friend of mine!"

"Who?"

Mackenzie was so excited to see Tommy, she responded hurriedly. "You don't know him, his…"

"What?" Miguel yelled!

She could tell that it pissed him off, but she couldn't wait to tease him later on! "Miguel, trust me." Tommy beeped the horn at Mackenzie and made a funny face. Mackenzie laughed and waved over at Tommy! "Miguel, everything is fine! I'll see you soon, bye!" Miguel was mad as hell, but he tried to keep his composure.

His friend José could tell that he was upset. "Miguel, you alright?"

"I'm good." Miguel looked at his watch and tweaked it a bit. "José, we are gonna make some good fuckin' money on this new business venture, trust and believe!"

Tommy and Mackenzie were eating ice cream at a parlor with their shopping bags at their sides. Mackenzie told Tommy everything that was going on between her and Miguel. "Mackenzie, he sounds nice, and he probably is. I just want you to be careful because it's still early in the relationship!"

"I know, Tommy, but this is real. I can tell it's real!"

"Girl, if you saw 'Puff-the-Magic-Dragon's- Ass' walking down the street, with the way you feel right now, you would think that Puff was *real*!"

Mackenzie laughed so hard! "Shut up! I'm serious! I know it's early, but you know what? Who is to say that this isn't real?"

"The Beast!"

"Girl, I know he loves me, Tommy!"

"-He better! What's not to love?"

Mackenzie lovingly smiled at Tommy, then heard her phone ringing. Miguel's name appear on the screen. "Hello?"

Miguel was mad as hell! "What's up?" He became even more infuriated with her as he listened to her cheerful-ass voice!

"Nothing much. Are you finished taking care of business today?"

"Yeah. Where you at?"

Mackenzie smiled at Tommy, making funny faces while trying her best to ignore Miguel's anger. "I'm out eating ice cream! When will you be back?"

"I'll be at the hotel in five minutes."

"Ok, I'll call you when I'm outside!"

"Alright." Click! Mackenzie just shook her head and laughed.

Tommy looked at Mackenzie. "What's wrong?"

"Nothing! We need to wrap this up so I can go meet up with him. What time are you hooking up with Mr. Starks?"

"Girl, he sent me a text while you were trying on that green dress at the Christian Dior Boutique! He is *expecting* me at four, so it's a good thing that The Beast called! Let's get out of here!"

As they drove down the street, Mackenzie sent Miguel a text that she was close to the hotel. Tommy pulled up his Mercedes SLR, compliments of Mr. Starks, to the hotel. Miguel was standing right outside the hotel waiting. Mackenzie saw Miguel and smiled, but Miguel just stood there, emotionless. Tommy put the car in park and waited for Mackenzie to exit first. Mackenzie took her time trying to think of what to say. She could tell that he was upset as she walked up to him, but she went ahead with her plan, anyway. She heard Tommy's door close and knew he was close behind her.

"Miguel, I want you to meet Tommy! He is one of my closest friends!"

Miguel did not even look at Tommy to say hello or nice to meet you. His eyes were fixed on Mackenzie. Tommy could see the fumes coming from Miguel's nostrils! He knew why Miguel was upset, so he turned to Mackenzie. "Girl, just stop trying to get an Oscar for that performance because it was HOR-I-BUL!" Miguel was baffled as he turned his attention to Tommy. Mackenzie smiled as Tommy put his hands on his hips, just like a woman would. "It is very nice to meet you, Mr. Miguel!"

Miguel shook his head and laughed! "It's nice to meet you too, Tommy! Any friend of Mackenzie's is a friend of mine!"

Tommy quickly turned toward Mackenzie. "Honey, I have to go! Mr. Starks will not like it if I'm late! Call me tomorrow afternoon. -Late afternoon! Oh, my goodness, don't forget your things!" Tommy ran over to the car like a woman trying to avoid stepping into puddles!

Mackenzie playfully rolled her eyes at Miguel. "Are you still mad at me?" Miguel just laughed! "No, no, no! I don't even want to hear that you're sorry!" They walked to Tommy's car and grabbed Mackenzie's bags.

Tommy waved at them. "It was nice meeting you, Miguel! Talk to you tomorrow, Mackenzie!" Tommy stood in his tracks and put his index finger on his temple, thinking of something. "Hmmm! Miguel and Mackenzie! M&M! -Just like those sweet chocolate candies! Look at y'all! All stuck together and whatnot!" Mackenzie and Miguel were laughing so hard! "M&M's I'll see y'all mañana!"

Mackenzie waved and yelled aloud, "Bye, girl! Be careful and be good!"

Tommy started up his convertible, "Girl, I ain't no damn E.T.! Beee gooood! Neverrrr!!! Holla' at your girl!" Mackenzie threw Tommy a kiss. "Luv ya, honey!" Tommy yelled, pulling off!

Miguel grabbed the bags, turned Mackenzie around, and tried to kiss her, but she pushed him away. Mackenzie walked toward the lobby! "I am so mad at you! You are on punishment!"

"What do you mean, punishment?" The both of them walked through the hotel lobby and arrived at the elevator.

Miguel walked up close to her once the elevator doors closed. "I missed you."

"You did? You sure didn't act like it when I got out of Tommy's car. How did it go today? Did you get a lot done?"

"Yeah, I did." The elevator doors opened, and they walked toward their suite. Mackenzie opened the door and closed it behind Miguel after he placed the bags on the floor. Mackenzie opened her purse and pulled out the money that he gave to her. He saw what she was doing and went over to her. "What are you doing? Don't be giving me change!" Mackenzie laughed while placing all of his money on the table. Miguel went behind her and kissed her on the back of her neck.

"No! Nope! I am officially mad at you!"

"No, you're not!"

Mackenzie pointed her index finger at him. "Well, I am officially disappointed in you for being mad at me for no reason!"

"No reason? I thought you were going out with a girlfriend!"

"I did!"

They both laughed, "Mackenzie, you know I didn't know that!" Miguel kissed her neck. "I'm taking you to dinner in about an hour. You want to get ready?"

"Yes!" Mackenzie took off her shirt, exposing her cream lace bra right there in front of him. She then pushed her shorts down, revealing her cream lace hipsters to match! Mackenzie stepped out of the shorts and walked up to Miguel, who was practically drooling. "Where are we going for dinner?"

"A friend of mine has invited us to dinner. They'll be here in an hour to pick us up."

Mackenzie kissed him. "Show me how much you missed me."

Miguel smiled and picked her up. "You are everything I need! Do you know that?"

"Show me."

"I will… now and real soon."

"Don't start talking that bullshit to me! You know I can kick your ass, right?"

"What?! Woman, your ass is truly crazy if you believe that shit!"

"Yes! I am crazy!"

"Yeah! You're crazy in love with me, aren't you?"

Mackenzie stuck her tongue out at him. "Yes, I am! I can't help it! What am I supposed to do?"

"You're supposed to keep on loving me just as much as I love you!" Miguel kissed her and laid her on the bed. "I feel like I've been away from you for longer than a day!" He laid beside her, and she laid her head on his chest while holding him. "This shit *is* a little scary, Mackenzie."

"I know how you feel!" They stayed there for a while, just thinking. No talking, just silence. Mackenzie nodded off to sleep, but Miguel did not. He just laid there trying not to love her too much, if that was at all possible. Miguel chuckled to himself, thinking about the actual possibility of not loving someone too much! He was sprung, and it felt good! Miguel felt like he was really on top of the world!

Chapter 6 - Surprises

Miguel reached down and kissed her. He took her bra off and sucked on her breasts. Miguel moved down to her stomach while she was still asleep. His excitement grew even more! Miguel pulled off his pants and underwear and laid on top of her. Mackenzie still didn't budge. He kissed and sucked on her neck and breasts some more before he entered her body. Mackenzie's eyes opened instantly, and Miguel chuckled! "I missed you."

"I missed you too." Mackenzie glanced at the clock over by the night table. "Miguel, we don't have that much time left." Miguel kept going faster, holding her onto her waist as he positioned himself on his knees. Mackenzie pulled her upper body up while he sat on his rear end so that she was now sitting on his lap! Both of them sat upright and moved with such intensity. They talked, kissed, and laughed while making love.

Miguel extended his legs and let Mackenzie ride him for a bit. Mackenzie then turned around while he was still inside of her. She rode him backwards and Miguel loved every ounce of her ass jumping up and down! After about fifteen minutes, he couldn't take it anymore! Miguel held on to her waist and carefully sat up, making sure that they stayed connected. Mackenzie simultaneously adjusted to his position and got on her knees. He started fucking her from behind, fast, and hard. "Miguel, you are going to make us late!"

"So, what!" Five minutes later, he came inside her! Miguel kissed her on the back and jumped up to get in the shower! Mackenzie laughed, trying to catch her breath. Miguel joined in her laughter. "You better get up or you're going to make us late!" Twenty-five minutes later, Miguel was ready! "Mackenzie, the driver just called. He's downstairs. Are you ready?" Mackenzie came out of the room rubbing shea butter on her hands, making sure she moisturized them well! "Mackenzie, you're gorgeous!" Mackenzie had on a Shoshanna One Shoulder Silk Black Dress, black heels, and a black evening purse. She pinned her hair up since she didn't have time to do it!

"And you are handsome as ever, especially in that suit! Oh, my locket!" She immediately ran into the room, grabbed the locket off of the counter in the bathroom, and walked to where Miguel was standing.

Miguel smiled as she fumbled with the lobster clasp. "Here, let me do it!" He leaned against her backside and put the necklace around her neck.

Mackenzie sighed! "Miguel, you smell so good!"

Miguel inhaled her scent. "So do you! There, now let's get moving."

Mackenzie played with her updo! "Do you have your wallet and room key?"

"Yes." Miguel took her hand, walked out of the room, and headed for the elevator. While in the elevator, each one put the finishing touches on the other as if they had been married for years! Mackenzie straightened out the collar on his suit jacket while Miguel smoothed out her backside!

They walked outside of the hotel toward a man who was standing outside of a black tinted Suburban SUV. The man smiled at Miguel. "Hello, Mr. Conway. It's good to see you!"

"It's good to see you too! Pete, this is Ms. Davids!"

"Good evening Ms. Davids!"

"Hi, Pete!" Pete opened the door for Mackenzie and closed the door behind her. Miguel walked to the other side and let himself inside. Pete entered the SUV and began driving.

Miguel settled himself and looked toward the front of the truck. "So, Pete?"

"Yes."

"I didn't have time to ask you earlier! How've you been?"

Pete laughed, "I've been doing well! How about you?"

"I've been doing great!"

Pete scrutinized him in the rear-view mirror. "I have never seen you this relaxed and content before!"

Miguel smiled, "It's all Ms. Davids' fault!" Mackenzie kissed him and wiped the lip gloss from his lips. "So where to tonight?"

"Bal Bay."

Miguel sounded as if he wasn't surprised. "Oh, ok. How many people?"

"Maybe seven."

Mackenzie nudged his arm. "Miguel, where are we going?"

"We're going to my friend's house for dinner instead of a restaurant."

"What's your friend's name?"

"José." Miguel felt a little tense and inquired further, "Pete, who else is coming?"

"No one new."

Mackenzie kept on with her interrogation. "How did you meet José?"

Miguel briefly scanned the outside of his window and then to Mackenzie. "I grew up with José in New York. We used to play basketball every day after school! When I moved to Philly, he moved to Florida."

Mackenzie changed the subject. "You know what? What do you have planned for your birthday next week?"

"Why?"

Mackenzie heard the dryness in his tone, but kept on smiling. She wanted to keep the conversation light. "Dag, I just wanted to know what you were doing! I didn't mean to pry!"

"I usually go to Vegas with the boys."

"Oh ok! I know y'all are going to have fun!"

Miguel tried to take the focus off him. "What do you want to do for your birthday?"

"I'm not even thinking about my birthday." Mackenzie's phone rang, and she peeped to see who was calling. It was her aunt, "Hi Auntie!"

"Hey, honey, how are you doing?"

"I'm fine. How are you?"

"I'm doing good! When I talked to you the other day, I forgot to ask you to call Stacy. She's going through so much right now, and she needs someone to talk to."

Mackenzie took a deep breath. "Ok, auntie, let her know that I'll call her tonight, ok?"

"Ok! After you talk to her, call me, and let me know how it went!"

Mackenzie picked with her nails. "Ok, I'll talk to you later!"

"Alright, bye!"

Mackenzie locked her phone and turned her head so that she could see the view from her window. She loved her family, and she was thankful that she had one. It was just that since she was a professional therapist, they also designated her as the *family* therapist! Mackenzie was the one who helped everyone within the family with their issues, but no one was really there for her own.

Mackenzie's mother and father both died in a car accident. After they died, her aunt took care of her. Although she didn't have any sisters or brothers, she had a few close cousins, two best girlfriends, and, of course, Tommy! Mackenzie had people in her life

whom she loved. She just didn't have anyone who was just there for

her! Her heart longed for that loyal companion for so long!

Mackenzie didn't realize that her aching heart forced a tear

or two to fall from her eyes. "Mackenzie, are you ok?"

"Yeah!"

Miguel turned toward her. "What happened?"

She tried so hard to smile so that she could stop thinking

about it. "Nothing. I was just thinking about something, that's all."

Mackenzie wiped the corner of her eye.

"Mackenzie, look at me!" Mackenzie turned around as he

commanded. "What were you thinking about?"

She took a deep breath. "My parents."

Miguel held her close. "They wouldn't want you to be upset

right now, baby. Your parents would want you to enjoy yourself!"

"I know. I know." She laid her head on Miguel's chest and closed her eyes. Miguel just rubbed her back until they arrived at José's.

Miguel got out of the SUV first and then helped Mackenzie. "See you at dinner, Pete!"

Pete waved his hand. "Ok!"

Mackenzie spotted the house. "Miguel, this house is…"

"I know! It's crazy huge!" Mackenzie turned around and looked out at the ocean. The water was majestic! She just felt like running out there and doing a cannonball! Miguel was talking to someone, but the ocean was calling her. Mackenzie walked toward the ocean and focused on its magnetic waves and the soft breeze that was trying to sweep her away! Miguel and José saw that the view captivated her. They walked over to her so Miguel could introduce them. "José, this is the woman in my life!" Mackenzie was smiling from ear to ear. She then turned around to José.

José was astonished! "Mackenzie? Mackenzie from NYU?"

Mackenzie grasped her chest. "Yeah! Oh, my gosh! Trevor?"

José reached over and gave Mackenzie a friendly hug. "How have you been?"

Mackenzie couldn't believe it! "I've been great, thanks to this man!"

Miguel smiled at the both of them. "So, when did you all meet?"

José told the story. "I met Mackenzie in my sophomore year! I was trying to go out with her, but she was not having it!" Mackenzie laughed. Miguel's smile dissipated. José could see that other people were entering the house. "Let me greet the others! Mackenzie, it is so good to see you again! Miguel, I'll see you all at dinner."

Miguel grabbed Mackenzie's waist and kissed her. José turned back around, saw Miguel kissing Mackenzie, and hurried in the other direction. Miguel kissed her neck. "You met him in college, huh?"

Mackenzie wiped the lip gloss from Miguel's lips. "Yeah! He was a big player on campus. Tommy had a huge crush on him. He was a nice guy and all, it was just something about him that didn't appeal to me." Mackenzie laughed. "I just cannot get enough of you! You know what? I think I know what it is!"

"What?"

Mackenzie made a funny face and put her hands on her hips! "Earlier! You left me hanging!" He frowned his face at her and then realized what she meant!

Miguel clapped his hands. "You are right!" He took her hand, and they walked toward the front entrance of the house laughing like kids at a playground!

They walked closer to José and the other guests. José stopped them. "Miguel, you know Paul and his wife, Yvonne."

"Yes. Hey! Good to see you! This is Mackenzie. Mackenzie, this is Paul and Yvonne." Everyone extended their greetings. Miguel wrapped up the introduction. "Excuse us!" Mackenzie held onto Miguel's arm while they walked toward the stairs, laughing.

José's envy of their involvement and apparent intimacy made him feel uneasy. "And where are you all off to?"

"The restroom." Miguel said, holding her hand while walking up the stairs. José couldn't say anything else without making himself appear to be an asshole! Miguel and Mackenzie entered the bathroom while Miguel locked the bathroom door behind them. He picked her up, put her on the vanity, pulled her thong to the side, and started eating her pussy! When he heard her moaning, he stopped. "Shh!"

"Ok!" He kept eating, and she tried to stay silent but couldn't! Miguel unbuckled his pants while he sucked and licked all over her pussy. She pulled his face up to hers and they kissed like they were starving for one another! Miguel pulled his pants down and quickly entered her. Mackenzie let out a sigh of pure bliss! They moved in sync with each other, smiling and laughing while enjoying their physical union.

"Mackenzie, let's make a deal."

"Ok!"

Miguel slowed down. "At the end of the summer, I want you to come and live with me."

"Miguel, that's in about two months!"

"What do you say?" Miguel kissed and sucked on her neck while moving inside of her.

"Maybe we should talk about it some more later on."

Miguel stopped moving. "I am sure. At the end of the summer, I want you to live with me!"

Mackenzie stayed silent for a moment. "What about my house?"

Miguel moved faster. "What about it?" Mackenzie couldn't think! She moaned as Miguel kept drilling deeper and deeper! Her high-pitched moaning pushed him closer to the edge. He kissed her lips, trying to keep down the noise but trying to keep her quiet excited him even more! Miguel felt it coming!

Mackenzie leaned back and wrapped her legs around his waist. She was getting flustered because she couldn't get comfortable on top of the vanity. "Put me on the floor!"

Miguel picked her up off the vanity and shimmied over to the rug. Mackenzie cracked up laughing as he laid her on the floor. José walked through the hallway when he heard some laughter coming from the bathroom and realized who it was. Miguel kissed her knee and calf as he held her leg straight up in the air. "Oh, God! Miguel! Please!"

Miguel moved deeper and faster inside of her! "Mackenzie, answer me! You gonna stay with me?"

"Yes!"

"You ready, baby?"

Mackenzie was in a daze! "For what?"

"For me!"

"Yes!"

José listened in the hallway and was getting a little excited himself.

The way Mackenzie moaned and moved her body, Miguel knew she was almost there! "Miguel! Miguel! Ohhh!"

Feeling Mackenzie's insides quiver while crying out his name, just intensified his orgasm! Miguel kissed her and let his come ooze inside of her. "Damn!"

Mackenzie giggled. "Was it a lot?"

Miguel lovingly kissed her lips. "You'll see when you get up!"

José took a few steps away from the bathroom door. His face turned beet red as he marched down the hall toward the back stairs.

Ten minutes later, Miguel and Mackenzie walked down the main stairs toward the dining room, where everyone was seated. Miguel considered the placement of the seating arrangements. There were two seats left. José positioned their seats diagonally across from one another. One chair was next to José, and the other was next to Paul. Miguel walked Mackenzie to the chair that was positioned close to Paul and pulled out her chair. As Miguel sat down next to José, the servers were bringing in the soup and salad.

Yvonne smiled like a cunning rat. "So, Mackenzie! What do you do for a living?"

"I'm a therapist for the Veteran's Administration. And when I am not being swept up off of my feet by my dear friend Mr. Conway, I organize different social workshops in my community."

Yvonne cleared her throat. "A therapist's salary isn't really…"

Mackenzie knew exactly where she was headed. "I know. The average salary isn't that rewarding. But to be honest with you, Yvonne, I'm not doing this for the money. When you have helped a soldier, who has put his or her life on the line to serve their country, it's an honor for me to help them get back on their feet. Don't get me wrong! Money is important, but when *you are only living* to make money, that's when problems arise. Don't you agree?"

Miguel just smiled while savagely eating his salad. José paid close attention to the conversation and remained silent. Paul subtly eyed Yvonne to stop, but she ignored his exasperation.

Yvonne kept trying to demean Mackenzie. "Yes, I do. Are you from Philadelphia?"

"Yes, are you from Philly, too?"

"No, I am from New Jersey, but I have friends that live in Chestnut Hill. Where do you live?"

Mackenzie took a fork full of her salad and looked at Yvonne while chewing her food. "I live in West Philly over by Cobbs Creek."

"Wow! Over that way!"

Mackenzie had an instant attitude, but knew how to play. "Yes, why did you say it like that?"

"Oh, no reason!"

Mackenzie knew exactly where she was coming from and dealt with her ignorance accordingly! "Yvonne, yes, I live in the hood, and I love it! My neighbors are eighty percent senior citizens. The other twenty percent are around my age, with families of their own. I don't have to worry about any of them trying to kill me, rob me, or harm me in any kind of way. We all take care of each other! We are a community."

Yvonne bobbed her head in the most snobbish way possible! "So, I guess you live there to help the community, not because you couldn't afford to live elsewhere, right?"

Paul couldn't take her blatant disrespect anymore! "Yvonne, what is wrong with you?"

Miguel just smiled!

José reached over to Miguel, "Miguel, aren't you going to say something?"

"Nope!" Miguel said, laughing. He had much confidence in Mackenzie's debating skills!

Mackenzie smiled. "Yvonne, what do you do for a living?"

"I'm an art dealer!" Yvonne said, being a real snobby-ass-bitch!

Mackenzie smiled and took a sip of her wine. She kept her voice steady. "This is my first time meeting you and yet you're trying to put me down. So, let's cut to the chase!"

"Ok!" Yvonne sneered.

Mackenzie raised her right eyebrow. "What is your net worth?"

Yvonne wrinkled up her face and crossed her arms on the table. "Well, I made…"

Mackenzie redirected her! "Honey. You asked me questions, and I answered them. A simple answer will do. What is your net worth? How much money do you have? You know, with all your assets?"

Yvonne felt the heat. She took a sip of her wine. "Why are you asking me that?"

"If you think you are so much better than me, it should be no real reason why you would have a problem answering the question."

Miguel, José, and Paul were following their conversation closely.

Yvonne took the defensive route. "I don't see why that is any of your business!"

Paul was embarrassed with Yvonne's behavior. She could see it all in his eyes. Yvonne turned her gaze over to Mackenzie and lightened up a little. "Mackenzie, I'm just saying that if you are like that, then…"

"Like what? I haven't given you or anyone in this room the impression that I'm like this or that!" Mackenzie chuckled! "You just met me about thirty minutes ago and all I said was hi! Now, you are judging me because I choose to live amongst those whom I feel comfortable with." Mackenzie kept her cool and was truly trying to educate Yvonne.

"I just don't understand that if you have it, why do you live in the hood?" Everyone turned their heads to Mackenzie except Miguel, who was now finishing his soup!

Mackenzie shook her head at Yvonne, who was not getting it at all! She smiled at José. "Trevor, what is your net worth?"

José did not hesitate. "About fifty million."

Mackenzie turned her head so that she could see her eye to eye. "Yvonne, it's not that difficult. What is your net worth?"

Yvonne took another sip of her wine. "Three hundred thousand dollars. What is your net worth?"

José interrupted and tried to calm everyone down, "Ok everybody! Let's just eat dinner and try to enjoy ourselves!"

Paul agreed. "Yeah, the food should be coming in shortly!"

Mackenzie took a sip of her wine. "Yvonne, I'm worth roughly sixty million dollars." Yvonne, Paul, and José stared at Mackenzie while Miguel shook his head. Mackenzie took another fork full of her salad. "Baby, how was the soup?"

Miguel busted out laughing uncontrollably. "It was good. Try some!" Mackenzie couldn't help but join in the laughter!

José laughed and nodded at Miguel. "Hey, did you all get lost finding the bathroom or what?"

Mackenzie was tired of all of them acting stuck-on-stupid. "You know Trevor, *sometimes* you can get lost trying to find the bathroom. But what's even more exciting is how you can get lost while *in* the bathroom!" Miguel winked at her while she puckered up her lips to him!

After dinner, they all went outside and sat by the pool. Mackenzie sat in between Miguel's legs and leaned her back against his chest while Paul, Yvonne, and José sat in separate beach chairs.

Miguel rubbed Mackenzie's arms while Paul talked to everyone about him and Yvonne, traveling to Aruba in a couple of days.

Yvonne felt like an imbecile and tried to be cordial. "Mackenzie, I'm sorry for my behavior at the dinner table."

"Apology accepted. Miguel, do you want some dessert?"

"Yeah! I want something sweet."

Mackenzie tapped José. "Trevor, do you have any ice cream, cake, or pie?"

"Yeah, I'll show you to the kitchen."

Mackenzie mumbled something under her breath and although Miguel heard her say something, he didn't catch what she said. "Mackenzie, what's wrong?"

"I'm tired of walking in these shoes!"

Miguel sat up! "Turn around." Mackenzie turned around and Miguel took her shoes off.

Yvonne tried again, feeling defeated. "Those shoes are pretty! What kind are they?"

"Payless!" Mackenzie said sarcastically. Miguel and Paul laughed as José walked Mackenzie to the kitchen.

José pulled out some bowls and spoons! "Mackenzie, it sure has been a long time!"

"Yeah, it has! So why haven't you married?"

"Why haven't you?"

"I'm waiting for the right man!"

José raised his eyebrow. "And I haven't come by the right woman yet!"

Mackenzie viewed his extravagant kitchen. "I hear that! Trevor, your house is beautiful!"

José opened the freezer and put the ice cream on the table. "Thank you! So, it seems like you and Miguel are hitting it off well!"

"Yes, I would like to think so!"

José paused for a moment and just stared at Mackenzie. "Miguel and I have seen our fair share of women over the years. Do you think you can keep his interest?"

Mackenzie's nostrils flared up and her head instantly tilted to a forty-five-degree angle. "What the hell are you talking about?"

José tried to get closer to her, but she stepped back. "Mackenzie, I am sorry. I did not mean it like that! I just want the best for the both of you, that is all."

Mackenzie stared at José, who seemed to be genuine about his apology. She took a deep breath and exhaled. Mackenzie fixed Miguel's bowl of ice cream and tried to calm down. "It's cool! Guess what? Remember Tommy?"

José squinted his eyes and then widened them. "Yeah, I remember."

Mackenzie laughed. "We still keep in contact!"

"Get out of here! How is he doing these days?"

"Tommy's good! I spent time with him this afternoon! He lives here in Florida!"

"Damn! It's a small world!" Mackenzie took the bowl and headed for the pool. José gently grabbed her arm and stared at her awkwardly. "I mean it, Mackenzie. I am sorry for what I said. It's just that I don't want you to get hurt."

"Trevor, thanks for caring, but I'm a big girl now." She smiled and walked back to where they were sitting. Mackenzie sat in between Miguel's legs again while he ate his ice cream.

~

An hour later, Mackenzie and Miguel were ready to leave. Morgan stood up and politely waved at Paul and Yvonne. "It was nice meeting you all."

"It was nice meeting you too, Mackenzie!" Paul said kindly. Yvonne finally kept her silence!

José, Miguel, and Mackenzie walked to the front door of the home. Pete pulled up the Suburban in front of Mackenzie and Miguel while they said their goodbyes. Mackenzie hugged José. "Trevor, it was good seeing you again after all these years!"

Miguel shook José's hand. "Thanks, man! Dinner was delicious as usual!"

José regarded them both. "When are you all leaving?"

"Tomorrow." Miguel answered, looking at his watch.

José looked at Mackenzie and smiled strangely. He then returned his focus to Miguel! "Maybe we all can do lunch tomorrow before you all head out!"

Miguel wrapped his arm around Mackenzie's waist, "I'll call you tomorrow and let you know." Mackenzie and Miguel got in the SUV and Pete drove off. When they arrived at the hotel, Miguel and Mackenzie said goodbye to Pete and went up to their suite.

Mackenzie dropped her purse on the chair in the bedroom. "Can you believe Yvonne trying to get all in my damn business?"

"She was just jealous."

"No! She was a snobby ass whoremonger!"

Miguel laughed while he took his shoes off. "Yeah, that too! When you told her that lie about being worth all that money, she looked like she wanted to shit in her pants!"

"What if I wasn't telling a lie?"

Miguel kept laughing. "Babe, come on! Let's go for a walk on the beach and take a bath."

"Oh, so you feel the same way as Yvonne, huh?"

"Mackenzie, if you have millions, good for you." He walked over to her and picked her up. "I want to take a bath right now!" Mackenzie laughed as he threw her on the bed.

"Miguel, what kind of business are you in with, Trevor?"

Miguel kissed her nose and tried not to answer her. "Why?"

"Because I want to know."

"I don't want to talk about business right now."

"Well, when would you like to talk about it? You are always evading the subject!"

"I'll talk to you about it when we get to Philly."

"Alright! Just don't let it be too long!"

"Who are you talking to?" Miguel started tickling Mackenzie. She was laughing so hard, Miguel had to laugh with her! When he stopped tickling Mackenzie, his phone fell out of his pocket and onto the bed. Mackenzie saw his phone displaying the name Trina on it. She handed him the phone and couldn't ignore reading the brief notification message that was displayed at the top of his screen.

José told me you were here! I've missed you! Call me!

Mackenzie put the phone in his hand. "Here you go." She stood up and made her way to the bathroom while shaking her head. Miguel unlocked the phone, read the message, and threw the phone on the bed.

"Mackenzie, what's wrong?"

"Miguel, nothing's wrong."

"I didn't call her!"

"Miguel, I didn't say that you did. I can't expect you to change your whole life because you met me!"

"Mackenzie?"

Mackenzie smiled and ended the conversation. "Miguel, it's cool!" She kissed him on the cheek, went into the bathroom, and closed the door. Mackenzie clenched her chest and turned on the water to fill the whirlpool. She started tearing up, thinking of how she had been living a fantasy over the past week.

Miguel had too many women, and she knew it! She thought about what Trevor said to her in his kitchen. Mackenzie nodded her head, realizing that it would only be a matter of time before the magic wore off and his eyes would wander. Plus, when she thought about it, what have they shared in the past week that he has never shared with another?

She knew her feelings were true, but there was no way of knowing if he was truly sincere, except to see it through. Staying until the end meant possible, excruciating pain. Mackenzie thought about her choices and felt that she had no choice but to let it ride out! She loved him! If it didn't work out, at least she could say that she gave it an honest shot! Mackenzie wiped her eyes in the mirror. She went over to the glass window to view the ocean while the water ran in the whirlpool. Mackenzie heard the bathroom door open, but she didn't turn away from her gaze.

Miguel walked up to her and held on to her from behind. "Mackenzie, I can't control who calls me."

"I know. I said it's cool."

"It doesn't seem like it."

"Miguel, just like there are men who call me, I know that there are women who still call you." Mackenzie pointed to the water. "It's so beautiful out there."

"Let's get in and go out to the beach."

"Ok." Mackenzie pulled away and went into the bedroom to get her things together for her bath. She heard her phone vibrating and remembered that she needed to call her cousin. Mackenzie answered the phone and forgot to see who was calling! "Hello?"

"Hey Mackenzie, it's Simon!" Mackenzie turned around and Miguel was staring right at her.

"Hey, what's going on?"

"Nothing much. I just came into town about an hour ago and I wanted to know if we could hook up and get a late dinner or some dessert."

"You know what, I'm actually out of town and I won't be back until late tomorrow."

"Well, I'll be here until next Friday, so I'll catch up with you later on in the week! Awe man, I'm going through a tunnel! I'm sorry, I'll call you right back." Simon's phone cut off and good thing it did because Miguel's ass was all over her. She paid him no attention and called her cousin like she said she would. Stacy's voicemail came on and Mackenzie left her a message. Mackenzie put her phone on the dresser and finished getting her things ready for bed. Miguel just sat in a chair in the bedroom while Mackenzie got herself situated.

She walked into the bathroom and turned off the water. Mackenzie's phone vibrated, but she couldn't hear it vibrating on the dresser from the bathroom. Miguel heard her phone, walked over, and grabbed it. The screen displayed the name Simon. He pressed the red phone icon, sending the call to voicemail. He then searched through her messages. Mackenzie walked to the doorway and just stood there, watching him. Miguel looked up from the cell phone and saw that Mackenzie was watching him. Mackenzie didn't say a word!

Miguel felt childish and shrugged his shoulders like a kid. "Here's your phone!"

She took the phone and put it back on the dresser. "Our bath is ready." Mackenzie pulled her thong down and put it with her things. Miguel walked over to her. "Mackenzie, what are you going to do about Simon?"

"Miguel, what do you mean?"

"Are you going to tell him to stop calling you?"

"Are you going to tell your female friends to stop calling you? Miguel, you can do whatever you want to do! *We* can do whatever we want to do! If you feel you want to talk to other women on the phone or take them out to dinner, movies, or whatever, just tell me! I would rather have you be upfront with me than lie about something that could ruin our friendship!"

"Mackenzie, I don't want you talking to other men anymore."

"I can understand that, but will you be talking to other women? You know what? How about we just keep it the way we originally decided until we get to where we can say, I am officially done!"

Miguel couldn't believe what she was suggesting! "Ok." She walked back to the bathroom and Miguel followed. They took the rest of their clothes off and sat in the tub. Mackenzie leaned back against Miguel's chest while he just held on to her. While they were in the tub, they kept the talking to a minimum. They just wanted to enjoy their intimate moment, discussing no one or anything else. After the bath, they massaged each other down with coconut oil. They were so relaxed that instead of going out, they laid in the bed and watched *V for Vendetta*. Thirty minutes into the movie, Mackenzie fell asleep. Miguel followed shortly thereafter.

~Sunday 4:36 a.m.~

Mackenzie felt Miguel sucking on the back of her neck. She was lying on her side, and he was directly behind her. The black satin nightgown that she was wearing was pulled up from her thighs to gain access! Mackenzie put her hand on his hip, permitting him to proceed. Miguel slid in between her legs and Mackenzie obliged!

~ Sunday 9:17 a.m. ~

Miguel woke up alone in bed. Mackenzie left him a note on the night table:

Good morning! I'm at the gym! I'll see you soon.

Miguel got up and knew just what he wanted to do while she was out. He first went to the bathroom and checked his phone. There were eight missed calls: two calls were from Cindy, three from Trina, one from Tasha, and two from his sister, Heather. Miguel called Heather back while getting himself together. "Hey! What's up!"

Heather squealed! "Hey!! What's up with you?"

"Nothing much. I'm in Florida."

"How's José?"

Miguel laughed at her excitement. "He's alright. What's going on with you?"

"I wanted to know if you were still coming up for my birthday."

"Yeah, but that's not until next month, Heather!"

"I know! I just wanted to check up on you."

"Awe! You love your brother, huh?"

Heather sucked her teeth! "Shut up!"

"Heather, when I come, I want you to meet my friend Mackenzie."

Heather teased Miguel! "Oh yeah? You already got your August chick set up? You huntin' early these days, huh?"

Miguel stayed quiet for a moment. "It's not like that this time."

Heather was quiet. She heard the seriousness in her brother's voice. "Oh! Ok! How is it with this one?"

Miguel took a quick breath. "I love her."

"Oh really? How did Tasha take that?"

Miguel laughed, thinking of the incident at the pool hall. "Tasha saw me with her!"

"What? What happened?"

"We were arguing. Tasha was about to leave, but she got in Mackenzie's face talkin' shit!"

"What happened?"

"She was acting stupid as usual, but as soon as she lifted her hand to do something, Mackenzie punched the shit out of her!"

"DAMMMNN!" Heather cracked up laughing. "That's what her dumb ass gets!" Miguel chuckled with Heather while he pulled out some clothes to wear. "Are you serious about loving her?"

"Yeah."

"Well, I'm happy for you! I'm glad that you finally found love. What are you going to tell all the rest?"

Miguel shook his head as if Heather were there in the room. "I've been ignoring them."

Heather shook her head too, as if Miguel could see her. "No! That ain't gonna work! Send them all a text message that you're not a single man anymore! If you don't tell them something, they're going to keep calling and coming at you!"

"I hear you. What do you want for your birthday?"

"Whatever. You know I'm easy to please."

"Speaking of pleasing, what's up with your boy, Dave?"

"He's ok. If he doesn't come correct on my birthday, it's a done deal! He's got to shit or get off the pot! I'll be twenty-three! I'm not getting any younger!"

Miguel laughed. "Yeah, you see how long it's taken me to find mine!"

Heather heard his tone! "So, you *are* serious about her, huh?"

"Yeah."

"Well, I can't wait to meet her! How old is she?"

"Old enough."

Heather snapped her fingers! "Maybe she can hang out with me while she's here!"

"I'll have to see about that one!"

"What?"

Miguel played off his seriousness. "I'm joking! I'm joking! How's grandma?"

"She's good! She said she can't wait to see you!"

Miguel couldn't wait to eat her cooking! "Tell her I'll call her later on tonight, ok?"

"Alright. I'll talk to you later this week!"

"Alright, later!"

~

Mackenzie ran three miles on the treadmill and worked on her abs, thighs, and arms. The sauna was just what she needed! She sat there for about ten minutes before going back to the suite. When Mackenzie walked in, she could tell that he wasn't there. There was a note on the fridge:

-I went out for a while. I'll be back!

Mackenzie jumped into the shower and knew exactly where she wanted to go! She was so excited! After showering and throwing some clothes on, she hopped onto the hotel shuttle. Once Mackenzie arrived at the store that she had in mind, she quickly picked out what she wanted, walked around for a bit, and then headed back to the hotel.

"Miguel? Phew! Good!" Mackenzie said, taking her sandals off. She smiled at the thought of taking a quick nap. Mackenzie opened her purse and unlocked her phone. She had five missed calls: one call was from Simon, one from Wayne, one from Tommy, one from Natalie, and one from an unknown caller. Mackenzie was hungry, but didn't want to get anything until Miguel got back. She put the phone back in her purse and watched TV until she fell asleep.

An hour later, Miguel walked in the door and put his bags down. "Mackenzie?"

"Yes." Mackenzie was in the bathroom, swishing mouthwash around in her mouth. Miguel picked up one bag and went into the bedroom. Mackenzie came out of the bathroom, went over to him, and gave him a hug and a kiss. "Hey baby, how are you?"

"I'm good! I went out and did a couple of things."

"Oh, ok! Did you eat yet?"

"No, I didn't."

Mackenzie walked over to her suitcase so that she could give him her surprise. "Good, because I'm starving!"

"Mackenzie, come here for a minute."

"Ok, I just wanted to get something real quick!" She said, bending over and grabbing hold of the box.

"Just leave it for a minute! Please!" She put the box back down, stood up, and turned to him while he held a box in his hands. "I have something I want to give to you." Her mouth dropped open wide as she shook her head from side to side at the medium-sized rectangular box. "Open it!" Mackenzie took the Tiffany box and opened it.

"Oh, my goodness! Miguel! It's beautiful!" He bought her a 2.71-carat diamond Tiffany Bracelet with beautiful round diamonds set in platinum. Miguel took it from the box and put it on her wrist.

"Do you like it?"

"Are you serious? Yes, I like it!" Mackenzie kissed him. "Why did you do this?"

"Because I love you!"

"Wait a minute!" She went over to her bag and pulled out a small square box. "This is crazy!" Mackenzie said, walking back to where he was standing.

Miguel looked disgusted. "What the hell is that?"

"What do you mean, what the hell is that? It's a damn box with your name on it!"

"I don't want it!" Miguel said, pushing it away.

"What did you say?"

"I don't do gifts from girls!"

"Well, I ain't no damn girl!" She walked up closer to him. "Miguel, I know plenty of FEMALES have bought you a gift over the years, so don't even act like that!"

"No, thank you! My birthday is next week! You can give it to me then!"

"Miguel, open this box before I step right on your damn toe!"

"Why you gotta get violent!" Mackenzie handed him the Bvlgari box. He opened up the box and just stared at it. Mackenzie bought him a 2-carat Bvlgari Griffe Round Diamond Stud set in 18 carats of white gold! It was sparkling like crazy! Miguel closed the box. "I can't accept that!"

"Why not?"

"It's too much!"

"So what? I bought it with my money! You only live once, and I love you! Why can't you accept this from the woman you love? It's not like I'm trying to buy you or anything! I saw it, I thought of your earring, and I wanted to, you know, upgrade you!" Miguel laughed! Mackenzie took his smaller earring off and put in the new diamond stud. "Do you like it?"

"Yes, I do! And don't buy me anything else!"

Mackenzie put her hands on her hips. "What about your birthday?"

"Well, ok, but after that, just special days, and holidays. I'm the only one who can buy major gifts outside the holidays!"

"Alright! But Miguel, what is a major gift?"

"-More than five hundred dollars!"

"Why?"

"Because I don't want you buying me gifts! I am the gift buyer!"

Mackenzie hugged him and stroked his ego. "Ok, so outside of the holidays and special days, I won't buy you anything that costs more than $500. Thank you so much for the bracelet." She kissed him on the cheek.

"Thank you!" Miguel kissed her on the lips.

Mackenzie sat on the bed and put her sandals on. "I am so hungry. Can we get something to eat?"

Miguel fiddled with his watch. "Mackenzie, next month I'm going up to New York for a couple of days."

"Ok. What day are you leaving?"

"August 1st."

She grabbed her purse and walked over to the kitchen area. "Please leave early! Are you driving?"

"Yeah."

"Ok. Again, please leave during the daytime. People drive so crazy in New York!" She took a bottle of water, opened it up, and took a sip.

Miguel stared at Mackenzie. "I want you to come with me. I want you to meet my grandma and my sister."

She shook her head while smiling from ear to ear! "You want me to meet the fam, huh? Are they waiting for me too, like Yvonne?"

Miguel laughed! "No, my family is straight! They're straight!"

"I'm just playing with you! Of course, I'll go with you. Just please remind me when we get close to the date!"

After having a quick bite to eat, they got their things together and headed to the airport.

Despite the delay in departing from Florida, everything was smooth sailing! They arrived at Philadelphia International Airport at 8:49 pm and hopped on the shuttle to take them to the parking lot. "Babe, you have your purse?"

"Yes, I have it. Do you have the keys?"

Miguel was tired. "Yeah, I have the keys." After pressing the unlock button on the key FOB, he put their bags in the trunk. Mackenzie just stood there, watching him. "What's wrong?"

She walked up to him and rubbed his arms. "Nothing. I just like looking at you, that's all!"

"Get in the car, woman." Mackenzie laughed and sat inside the car.

Miguel plopped into his seat and pressed the button to start up the car. He heard her phone vibrating against something inside her bag. Miguel stared at her while she checked her phone.

Mackenzie took a quick look at her phone and then at him. "What's wrong?"

"Nothing," Miguel said while turning on the radio. Keisha Cole's "Love" was playing on the radio and Mackenzie sang right along with Keisha! "Babe, you need to leave all that singing to Keisha Cole!"

"Shut up!" Mackenzie said, laughing. She noticed he was heading straight for Mt. Airy. "Miguel, why aren't you taking me home?"

Miguel rubbed his head and sighed. "You can't go to work from my house?"

"I don't think I have any dress clothes over there."

"Yes, you do!"

Mackenzie sensed his irritation. "No. Plus, I need to get a couple of things for work, and my truck is at my house."

"Alright." He changed lanes so that he could go back the other way to take Mackenzie home.

Mackenzie could tell that he was more irritated than before. "I know you're probably tired from the flight, carrying the bags, and now driving, but that's no reason to get upset!"

Miguel briefly closed his eyes and shook his head. "I'm not upset with you. It's just becoming a hassle, that's all! -Driving here and then back at my house!"

"Well, no one said that we had to go to your house! Why can't you stay at my house? That way you can leave out in the morning with me. I know my house isn't that big, but I have most of the amenities and appliances that you have!"

Miguel shrugged his shoulders. "You're right, let's go to your house." They pulled up twenty minutes later and parked right in front of the house. He took out the bags while Mackenzie opened the front door. Miguel dropped the bags on the enclosed porch while Mackenzie took her shoes off and entered her home.

Miguel didn't pay much attention to the interior of her home until now. He took a quick inventory while walking through the first floor. She had recessed lights installed in the living room, dining room, and kitchen. Miguel noticed the beautiful cherry oak hardwood floors, huge plasma T.V. on the wall, Bose stereo system, fireplace, plush leather furniture, candles, stainless steel appliances, huge fridge, built-in wall oven, ceramic flat top range, modern faucet, and fixtures throughout the house! He was impressed!

Mackenzie went upstairs to the back room and turned on the light while he followed. "This is my closet, so if you want to put your things in here, you can." Miguel was taken aback with her interior designing skills! Mackenzie transformed the bedroom into a custom-built modern closet. All of her clothes were hanging up and there were two huge bureaus in the middle of the room. Her shoes were organized by color and neatly placed on custom-built shelves against the back wall.

She walked down the hall and pointed to each adjacent room. "This is a room where I usually work and read. This is the guest room, that's the bathroom, and my room is over there. -And that's the end of your official tour! Like I said, I know it's smaller than what you're used to, but this is my home." Mackenzie smirked and walked into her bedroom.

Miguel went into the bathroom and closed the door.

Mackenzie turned on her television and got ready for the next day.

Miguel flushed the toilet and turned on the water to wash his hands.

He opened the medicine cabinet and saw Tylenol, Excedrin, Midol,

Band-Aids, Peroxide, Alcohol, a thermometer, vitamins, Pepto, Ex-

lax, and Visine. He pulled back the shower curtain to see that she

had all kinds of shower gels, scrubs, and bubble baths.

Miguel admired her attentional to detail. The elegantly

placed candles on tall pillars gave the small bathroom a luxurious

and warm feel. After washing his hands, he came out of the

bathroom. As soon as he arrived at her bedroom doorway, he could

see that Mackenzie was in some sort of distress! "Mackenzie, what's

wrong?"

Mackenzie shook her head from side to side. "Xavier died! It

was just on the news!"

"What?"

"He died in a motorcycle accident on 76," she said, holding

her head in her hands.

Miguel appeared to be surprised. "Wow!"

Mackenzie sighed and stared at the floor for a moment, thinking about Xavier. She broke her stare. "Can I get you something from the kitchen?"

"Yeah, sure! What do you have?"

"I have some vanilla, strawberry, peach, and coffee ice cream." Mackenzie responded, sounding like a robot.

"I'll take some strawberry ice cream."

"Ok." Mackenzie got up and walked toward the door.

Miguel came up behind her and held her. "Come here!" He laid her on the bed and wanted to get her mind off Xavier.

"Did you like Florida?"

"Yes, it was beautiful, especially when you were holding me on the beach. I will never forget that! You and Trevor growing up together was a genuine surprise too! What in the world is he into anyway with that big ass house?"

"He's a big investor."

"And what was he consulting with you about?"

Miguel shook his head. "No business talk tonight!"

"Whatever! Let me get your ice cream."

"How about we get some ice cream from Dairy Queen or some other ice cream place?"

"I know you're tired. We don't have to."

"I'm ok! Let's get some ice cream and take a walk down Kelly Drive."

"Ok."

~

While walking by the water, Miguel sat down and pulled Mackenzie to sit down on his lap. "You are one romantic man, you know that?"

"Yes!" Mackenzie slapped his arm and stood up. She leaned against a tall sculpture positioned near the water. Miguel stood up and went over to her. "How's your ice cream?"

Mackenzie tried to smile. "It's good! How's yours?"

"It's good. Mackenzie, if you want to talk about it, we can talk about it."

"Miguel, it's not like I loved Xavier or anything. It just reminds me of how alone I am." Miguel felt her pain and could see it all over her face. Mackenzie started tearing up. "See, you have a family and plenty of friends, male and female, but I don't! I mean, I have friends, but it's just me!"

"You are not alone anymore! You have me!" Mackenzie smiled as her tears fell from her face. "*I'm* here now!" Miguel kissed her. "I love you and soon you'll see just how much!" He kissed her again and wiped away her tears. "You are not alone anymore, Mackenzie, ok?"

"Ok."

"Have you thought about what you are going to do with your house?"

"No, I haven't."

"Take your time. There's no rush, ok?" Mackenzie shook her head yes. "Maybe I should go home for the night so you can have some time to yourself."

Mackenzie nodded her head, understanding his suggestion. "If you want to go home, I understand. It *has* been a long day."

"No, I'm just thinking about you."

"Miguel, I'm not throwing a guilt trip on you. If you want to stay, stay, but if you want to go, it's cool." Miguel's phone was vibrating. While he checked it, Mackenzie walked away. The call was from Cindy. He sent the call to voicemail and put the phone in his pocket.

Miguel went over to her. "It's just that you seem a little upset."

"Well! Make me feel better!" He stared at her and took her hand. They entered the car, and he sped away. Miguel arrived at her house in fifteen minutes. When she opened the front door, he picked her up, kicked the door closed, and took her to the bathroom. He ran the shower, took off all their clothing, and stepped into the shower. Miguel did not say a word to her. He just did what she requested! Miguel washed her body and his own. When he was done, he wrapped them up with towels, picked her up, and placed her on top of the bed.

Miguel opened her towel and started licking and sucking on her pussy so good that she started tearing up again. He saw her crying and lifted her head. "-You, ok?"

Mackenzie sniffled. "Where did you come from? Why are you here with me?"

"Why are you here with *me*?"

Mackenzie exhaled, "I love you." Miguel made love to her throughout the night and into the early morning.

~

Miguel got up and showered at around nine in the morning. While he was in the shower, Mackenzie got up, brushed her teeth, and washed her face. "Good morning."

Miguel peeked through the curtain. "Hey, baby! How do you feel?"

"I feel good! Are you going to work today?"

"Yeah! I have some things to take care of. You want to do dinner later on tonight?"

"Yeah, sure, let me get you another towel and toothbrush." Mackenzie took some toiletries from the guest room, put them on the vanity, and closed the door.

Twenty minutes later, Miguel wrapped the towel around his waist and entered her bedroom. "So, what are you going to do today, baby?"

"I'm not too sure! Since I took off from work, I'll probably run some errands." Miguel went downstairs and grabbed his bag. He took it upstairs and dressed in her back dressing room. When he finished, Miguel walked to her bedroom doorway and put his hands on each side of the entryway. Mackenzie just laid there with only the tennis bracelet and locket adorning her body. "Have a good day today and please be careful."

"I will. I'll call you later." He walked over to her and kissed her lips.

"Lock the bottom lock for me, please."

"Ok." He walked down the hall and down the stairs. Then he ran up the steps and walked back into the bedroom. Mackenzie opened her eyes to see why he came back. Miguel stopped in her bedroom doorway just like he did before. "I love you!"

Mackenzie sat up and stood in front of bed in her nakedness. Miguel slowly walked over to her. Mackenzie wrapped her arms around his neck and kissed him. "I love you too." He kissed her again and felt on her breasts. Mackenzie pulled away and laid back down on the bed. "I'll see you later on." Miguel smiled and kissed her on her nose.

~That next Friday: Miguel's Birthday~

Mackenzie packed up all her things and got herself ready to leave the office for the day. She made a few last-minute calls before seeing Miguel off for his birthday celebration in Vegas. Mackenzie then called him, "Miguel?"

"Hey baby, what time will you be here?"

"I'll be there in about thirty minutes, ok?"

"Alright, I'm just finishing up packing! The flight leaves at 8:15 and we're leaving at 6:30."

"Alright, who's there now?"

Miguel changed his watch. "Pretty much everybody!"

"Ok, I'm bringing my gift with me!"

"Alright!" Miguel shook his head, not wanting to hear about the gift that she had for him.

"See you in a little!"

"Baby? When I come back, I need to get your truck and get that maintenance taken care of."

"Ok, I'll see you soon!"

~ 6:18 pm ~

Mackenzie parked by Miguel's house and made a call from her truck. "Hi! Ok, in exactly five minutes, call me! Thank you so much!" Mackenzie grabbed her purse, got out of the truck, walked up to the door, and rang the bell to announce her entry. She was so excited as she opened the door! "Hey everybody!"

"Hey, Mackenzie!" Teo walked up to her and hugged her.

"Hey Teo, where's the birthday man?"

"He's in the kitchen having a drink."

Mackenzie playfully hit his arm. "How've you been?"

"Good, I can't complain!"

On her way to the kitchen, she talked to the guys, "Y'all ready to go, huh?"

They all cheered in unison! "Yeah, you know it!"

"There she is!" Yelled Miguel, smiling from ear to ear.

Mackenzie went up to him and kissed him. "Miguel, please promise me something!"

"What is it, baby?"

"Take care of yourself and be careful!"

"Baby, I will! Don't worry!"

"You promise?"

"I promise!"

Mackenzie's phone rang, and she answered it! "Ok! Thanks, bye!"

"Who was that?" Miguel asked with an attitude.

"I have a surprise for you! Come with me!" She held his hand and pulled him through the house to the front door.

Teo was wondering what was going on. "Mackenzie, what's wrong?"

Mackenzie laughed like a kid during Christmas! "Nothing, I'm about to give Miguel his birthday gift! Come outside!" Everyone followed Mackenzie and Miguel out to the front of the house. They stood there on the pavement, waiting.

Miguel laughed! "Mackenzie, what's going on?" *Honk, honk, honk*! A loud horn from an enormous truck sounded off from the end of the block!

Mackenzie laughed like a little kid. "I told you! I'm giving you your birthday gift!" A huge black truck pulled up to the curbside. Miguel stood there wondering what the hell was going on. Two men came out of the truck and waved at Mackenzie. She waved back and could not stop laughing.

Teo came over to where Mackenzie and Miguel were standing. "What are they doing?"

"You'll see!" Mackenzie said while smiling radiantly. The two men entered the back of the truck, and an electronic ramp came out of the back end. Just then, the two men walked down the ramp with a red Ducati 1198S.

"Yo' Mackenzie! Mackenzie!" Miguel yelled! "Oh, my God! Is that my fuckin' bike? Is that mine?"

"Yes! Happy Birthday," Mackenzie said, jumping up and down!

"Ahhhh," Miguel yelled while picking her up and kissing her lips! "You knew baby, you knew I wanted this! I never said it, but you knew I wanted it!"

Mackenzie handed him the key, with his initials engraved on the key chain.

They walked over toward the two men. "Congratulations Mr. Conway! Happy Birthday!"

"Thank you!"

"Ms. Davids, I need your signature here and here." Mackenzie signed the paperwork and handed both of them an envelope. They handed her a box with all the information that Miguel needed for the bike. "Thank you, Ms. Davids. Take care!"

"Thank you so much!" Her phone rang. "Hello? Yes, everything was perfect. Thank you so much! Ok, bye!" All his boys were gawking at the bike with Miguel. Mackenzie walked over to them. "Miguel, I'm going to head out! This box has everything you need for the bike. It has your Ducati Leather Jacket, title, registration, tags, insurance, handbook all that! Everything is in your name except the insurance. The insurance is under my name because I didn't want to get all your info. and ruin the surprise!" She kissed him. "I love you! Be careful and have fun!" Miguel just stood there staring at her with his astonished ass! He didn't know what to say! Mackenzie walked to her truck when Miguel asked Teo to hold the box.

Miguel followed behind her. "Mackenzie."

"Yes."

"Why did you do that?"

"It's your birthday! It's a gift from the heart! Now get ready for your flight. I love you!" She kissed him and sat in the truck.

Miguel was speechless! His mind was completely blown! "I can't believe you!"

Mackenzie winked her eye at him! "Believe it! Come back to me!"

Miguel kissed her forehead. "I'll call you later!"

He started walking away from her truck when she remembered, "Miguel!"

"Yeah!"

"It has a full tank of gas!" Miguel smiled and winked at her. She blew him a kiss and drove off. The bike was identical to the one that was on the cover of the magazine lying beside his bed and bookmarked all on the inside. Whenever they just chilled out in bed, he would read about the specs. Miguel couldn't believe that she bought the bike for him. He hadn't even talked to her about how badly he wanted it. She knew! Mackenzie paid attention to him and not to just what he said. No one had ever done that before.

Teo walked with Miguel while he put the bike in the garage. "Yo, Mackenzie really surprised you, huh?"

"Yeah, man. I still can't believe it!"

"Miguel, she must love you for real!"

"I know man, I know!"

Teo shrugged his shoulders, "I know it hasn't been that long, but so what? I could tell when I first met her that y'all were good!"

"I ain't even gonna lie, Teo! I love her!"

"Ain't shit wrong with that!" They both laughed and gave each other a pound. Teo quickly nudged Miguel's arm with an overly surprised expression on his face! "Yo, I heard your boy got squashed, huh?"

"Yeah! How 'bout that?" They both smiled while going inside the house.

Mackenzie was happy and relieved that Miguel was coming home. He called her twice on Friday night, and they talked about three times on Saturday. Mackenzie and her cousin Stacy left early in the day to do a little shopping at the King of Prussia Mall and to get some lunch. Stacy was in a quandary because her husband was ready for them to have children.

"Mackenzie, I'm just scared that during the pregnancy, he's going to act funny towards me. I'm going to gain all that weight and he'll probably start talking to other women and shit! I'm not trying to go through all that drama!"

Mackenzie walked out of the Neiman Marcus store with Stacy at her side. "Stacy, is Walt good to you?"

"Yes."

"Has he done anything in the past that would lead you to believe that he would do something like that to you?"

"No! Not really."

Mackenzie stopped walking and turned to Stacy. "So, do you think it's fair to say that these are your insecurities and not his?" Stacy was silent. "Stacy, we are all human. We live, feel, and learn. It's all good! Your feelings are normal! Do you think you're the only woman who has felt this way when their husband wanted children?" Stacy laughed. "Even though I've never been pregnant or had children, I understand how you feel! Talk to Walt and let him know how you feel! Don't talk to him about what you *think* he's going to do, but how *you feel*! Then, and only then, the both of you can decide when you all will start your family!"

Mackenzie's phone vibrated. She took it out of her purse and saw Miguel's name appear on the display. "Hello?"

"Hey Baby!"

Mackenzie smiled! "Hey, what's up?"

"Nothing much. We're about to get something to eat in a minute."

Mackenzie smiled, thinking that she was about to do the same thing. "Did y'all have a good time last night?"

Miguel looked at his watch. "Yeah, we did! I'll be there at around seven and I should be home around 7:30, 7:45."

"Ok."

"What time are you coming through?"

"Just call me in enough time for me to meet you there. Is that cool?"

"Alright, I'll see you later."

Mackenzie closed her eyes. "Alright, be careful!"

"Ok babe! I love you!"

"I love you too, bye!"

Stacy's face was full of surprise. "Mackenzie, who was that?"

Mackenzie shook her head and smiled while locking her phone. "That was Miguel!"

"Your man, huh? When are we going to meet him?"

"I'll bring him by soon." Mackenzie said, while putting things in their proper place within her purse.

"Where did you all meet? Does he have any children? How old is he?"

"Dag Stacy! Take a breath!" Mackenzie said, laughing. "We met out West, no he doesn't have any children, and he's old enough!"

"-And you are in love?"

"Yes, Mrs. Thang! I am in love! Enough about me. What are you going to do?"

"I'll talk to him like you suggested."

"Good, now let's eat!"

~7:18 p.m. ~

Mackenzie finished packing her bag and was fixing her hair in the bathroom mirror. After she finished up, Mackenzie took her bag downstairs and put it in the living room when her phone vibrated. Miguel had sent her a text message:

I'm just leaving the airport. I should be home by 7:40. I'll meet you at

the house!

She put the phone down and went back upstairs for some finishing

touches.

~ 7:57 p.m. ~

Mackenzie pulled up in his driveway. She stopped at the

market to get him an ice cream cake and candles before arriving at

his house. Mackenzie didn't know if they said happy birthday or not

while they were in Vegas, but she bought it anyway. She took her

slides off and put her heels on while sitting in the truck. After

grabbing her purse and the shopping bag, she walked up to the

house. Mackenzie rang the doorbell and Miguel quickly opened the

door. The both of them just stood there and stared at each other. "I

bought you an ice cream cake…"

Miguel kissed her mid-sentence and guided her into the

house. He took the bag out of her hands. "Wait here." Miguel

carried the cake to the kitchen and put it in the freezer while

Mackenzie waited by the door. Miguel came back to where she was

standing and picked her up. "I missed you so much!"

"I missed you too! Did y'all have a good time?"

"Yeah, we had so much fun!" He walked closer to her. "We gambled like crazy." Miguel unbuttoned her shorts and let them fall to the floor. He smiled at how she didn't have on any panties. Mackenzie had a bikini wax while he was gone, and he noticed! He grazed her pussy and couldn't believe how soft her skin felt. Miguel knelt on both knees and kissed her lips while inhaling her scent. Miguel stood up, pulled her shirt over her head, and marveled at her breasts. He stared at her body and grabbed her close. Mackenzie pulled back and sashayed to the kitchen with her high heels on!

"Where are you going?" Miguel asked, feeling a little light-headed.

"I'm thirsty! Since you didn't offer me anything to drink, I guess I can help myself!" Miguel admired the view from behind and shook his head. Mackenzie grabbed the container of orange juice and drank out of the bottle. Miguel stood there and watched the juice drip from her lips. She put the bottle on the counter. "Ahhhh!" Miguel went over to her and licked the juice that trickled down her mouth onto her chin and neck. Mackenzie moaned and kissed him. She could feel his dick poking her through his jeans.

Mackenzie pulled at his belt buckle and unbuttoned his pants. Miguel picked her up and put her on the island. She hopped right off, took his hand, and walked up to his room. When they walked in, she stooped down to the floor. Miguel took everything off and laid on top of her. Mackenzie kissed and sucked all over his neck.

Miguel entered her and moaned a sigh of relief that he was finally at home. "Baby, I missed you so much!"

"I missed you too!"

He slowed down. "Mackenzie, you gotta turn around for me!"

She got on her knees. "Why did you say it like that? What's wrong?"

"Nothing, I just need to fuck you!" Mackenzie kissed him and turned back around. Miguel was going strong for a good twenty minutes. Mackenzie came once and was coming up on the second.

"Mackenzie!"

"Yes!"

"You love me?"

"Yes!"

"You better, 'cause you're about to be pregnant!" Miguel mumbled! "-All this nut!" Mackenzie could feel that he was deep inside of her, and it felt so good! "Here it comes, baby, here it comes! Shit Mackenzie!"

"No! Not yet!"

"I can't hold it! Here it comes!" He moved fast and deep inside of her, shooting all of his semen inside. Mackenzie kept her head down, ass up, and came right along with him! "Baby, you all right?"

"Yes!" Mackenzie lowered her body to the floor and closed her eyes for a few seconds.

Miguel laid down beside her and kissed her. "I love you!" Mackenzie smiled and kissed him. She stood up and went to the bathroom to run a quick shower.

Mackenzie was so wet in between her legs that she just had to take one. Ten minutes later, Miguel appeared in the bathroom and entered the shower. "Hey, Mr. Conway!"

"Ms. Davids, what are you doing here?" Mackenzie laughed! She took her washcloth, lathered it with the soap, and washed all over her body. Miguel just stood there and watched. Mackenzie moved as if she was in the shower by herself. Miguel washed his body and when Mackenzie was about to get out of the shower, he grabbed and kissed her.

Miguel swiftly raised her leg and stuck his dick inside. Mackenzie kissed all over his face and neck. Miguel picked her up, and she held on to him while he made love to her against the shower wall! Her extremely wet pussy, along with her seductive moaning, led him to come quickly inside of her again.

~

After quietly relaxing on the bed for a while, they decided to go downtown for a quick bite to eat. Mackenzie went downstairs and brought her clothes upstairs so that she could get dressed. She searched in one of his drawers for a bra and a pair of panties. Miguel put on his pants when he heard his doorbell ring. He looked out the window. "What the fuck! Mackenzie, stay upstairs alright!"

"Ok."

Miguel put on his shirt and socks. He then ran downstairs to the front door. Mackenzie remained on the bed and listened to what was going on downstairs. Miguel opened the door, walked outside, and closed his front door behind him. "Cindy, why are you here at my house?"

"I've been calling you since you were in Florida, and you haven't returned my calls. Then the other day you sent me a text message about how you needed to talk to me!"

Mackenzie walked down the hallway toward the kitchen. She sat on the top step so that she could hear everything that was being said.

Miguel was so disgusted! "So, again, let me ask you! Why are you at my house? Whenever I wanted to see you, did I just come to your house without talking to you first?"

"No!"

Miguel lowered his threatening voice. "So again, why are you at my fuckin' door?"

"No, but..."

"But what?" Miguel yelled furiously. "You know the deal, Cindy! You fucking know! -And you gonna pop up at my fuckin' house! Why would you do that?"

"I was worried about you!"

"What?" Miguel calmed down and chuckled sarcastically! "Cindy, I can't mess with you like that no more, alright! That's what I wanted to talk to you about on the phone, or somewhere else, not at almost ten o'clock at night on my fuckin' doorstep!"

"Alright, well, that's all that you had to say!" Miguel just stood there. "Why are you looking at me like that?"

Miguel's repugnance was all over his face. "Why do you think?"

Cindy looked at the ground and then up at Miguel. "I'm sorry!"

Miguel wanted her to just fuckin' leave. "Me too."

"So that's it, huh?" Cindy looked at the house and then at him with teary eyes.

"Yeah, that's it."

"Can I have a hug?"

"No."

Cindy's tears kept on falling. "Damn, I can't even get a goodbye hug!"

Miguel took a deep breath and sighed. "No."

"Alright!" Cindy started walking down the driveway toward her car when she turned back! "Miguel, you take good care of yourself, ok?"

"-Yeah, you too." Miguel watched her as she walked to her car and drove off. Miguel sat on the step for a minute or two and then went back into the house. He plopped on the couch and blew out a mouthful of air as he laid his head back. Miguel thought about all the women he had and tried to think of how the fuck he was going to handle them all! Miguel thought about Heather's simple suggestion and did something similar. That way everybody would know without having to talk to them personally.

His phone vibrated. It was Nikki. He met her last summer, but kept in touch from time to time. Miguel sent it to voicemail and threw his phone on the other side of the couch. He put his head down in his hands and couldn't believe what had just happened. Mackenzie came down the living room stairs a few minutes later and sat on the loveseat by herself. Miguel knew she was sitting right across from him, but he didn't look at her. He just spoke. "You still want to get something to eat."

"No. We can just relax."

"I'm good. Let's go!"

"No, you're not."

"Yo', don't tell me how I'm feeling alright! I said I'm good!" Miguel said, raising his voice.

Mackenzie stayed calm. "If you're good, why are you yelling at me? I'm just trying to talk to you."

"I'm yelling at you because you're trying to make something out of nothing."

Mackenzie kept her composure. "I'm not trying to do anything. I'm just being understanding of this situation."

"Ok! Now you're making up shit! What situation do we have, Mackenzie? Huh? Tell me?"

Mackenzie raised both of her eyebrows and shrugged her shoulders. "Telling our friends that it's over."

"Mackenzie, please! You are going overboard with this shit!"

Mackenzie stood up and was tired of trying to diffuse his anger. "First, you need to stop talking to me like that! And if I'm going overboard, why is this the second female argument you've been in because you haven't told them it's over? And if you want to get technical, *my* friends are not hounding me like that because I'm not fucking them!"

Mackenzie went upstairs to get her things so that she could leave. She stomped her way back downstairs, grabbed her purse and keys from the kitchen, and headed for the front door.

Miguel stood up and threw his hands up in the air. "Where are you going?"

"Home!"

"What the fuck is your problem?"

Mackenzie just shook her head at him in disgust at the way he was cursing at her. "I'm not trying to hear you curse me out for wanting to just talk to you! If you needed a moment by yourself, you should have just said so! Don't get on me for trying to be understanding about what's going on! I have friends that are calling me and wanting to see me too! The difference is that I'm not fuckin' mine!" Miguel sat back down on the couch and just shook his head while staring at the floor beneath him. Mackenzie left out of the house and hopped in her truck. She drove to Kelly Drive and sat out there by the water.

Mackenzie wished her mom was still living. She wished she could just cry in her mother's arms. Instead, she pretended her mom was there, sitting by her side. Mackenzie accepted the fact that no matter how good things seemed to be, she would always end up being alone.

She knew she was feeling pretty bad because of the argument with Miguel, but she didn't want to feel depressed. Instead of allowing all of those negative thoughts to roam around in her head, she recalled joyous memories of her parents during her high school graduation, prom, and Disney World!

Mackenzie felt her phone vibrate. It was Miguel but, Mackenzie didn't answer. Her mind wandered to thoughts of prom night when her dad had tears in his eyes. Mackenzie's phone vibrated again, and it was Miguel. "Hello."

"Mackenzie."

"Yes."

"When are you coming back home?"

"You mean to your house?"

"Mackenzie, when are you coming back?"

"I don't know."

Miguel tried to hold back his anger. "How long is that?"

Mackenzie took a deep breath. "I'm just gonna stay at home for the night and get myself ready for work."

"Mackenzie, things just got out of hand. I shouldn't have gone off on you like that."

"Ok. I'll talk to you tomorrow."

Miguel sighed, "Alright."

Mackenzie ended the call and let the last of her tears fall while sitting out by the water. She stared out into the darkness for about a good twenty minutes before walking over to her truck. Mackenzie pointed the alarm device at the truck. Just then, Miguel walked over to the truck! Mackenzie stopped where she was standing with her blood-shot red eyes. "What are you doing here?"

Miguel's heart sunk deep into his stomach when he saw her face. "Mackenzie, can you please follow me to the house so that we can talk?"

Mackenzie raised her head toward the sky, trying to hold back her tears. "I don't feel like talking right now, Miguel."

"Can you just come to the house, then?"

"Miguel, I'll come over to talk, and then I'm going home."

"Alright." Miguel drove so fast that by the time Mackenzie pulled up to his house, the car was already parked. Mackenzie walked in and Miguel was sitting on the couch. He stood up, went over to her, hugged, and kissed her. "Mackenzie, I'm sorry, baby! You mean more to me than all of them put together. I'm ready to cut 'em loose." Mackenzie studied him closely and just stared at him. "I mean it! That's it, I'm done!"

Mackenzie spoke confidently, "You don't have to do this. It's your life. Do whatever makes you happy."

"I'm doing this because I want to give you my full attention and because I love you!" He gave her a big hug. "What are you going to do about your friends?"

"I'll just tell them I'm with someone else."

"That's all that you're going to tell them?" He said, playing in her hair.

"What else do you think I should say?"

"I want you to tell them I'm waxing that ass!"

Mackenzie was still upset, but gave him a partial smile. "Miguel, I'm going to head out, ok?"

"Why?"

Mackenzie rubbed her forehead. "I'm tired. I just want to go home and get in bed."

"Then go upstairs and rest while I get us something to eat."

"Miguel, I'm..."

"No!" Miguel held her close. "You're going to stay here with me!" He said, kissing her over and over. "We're going to have a light dinner, then we're going to have some dessert!" He said while kissing her again, making her smile! "Wait a minute! We have ice cream cake in the freezer, right?"

"Yes."

"So, where do you want to go?"

"It's your birthday weekend. You choose." Her phone started vibrating in her pocket. She reached in and saw that it was Simon.

Miguel enthusiastically clapped his hands and yelled, "Hell Yeah! -Contestant number fuckin' one! Go ahead baby, handle it! Handle that shit!" Miguel was laughing his behind off!

Mackenzie sat down on the loveseat and crossed her legs comfortably. "Hello?"

"Hey Mackenzie, how are you? I've been trying to reach you for the past couple of days!"

"I know. I've been crazy busy. Simon, I'm seeing someone right now. I won't be able to see you anymore."

Simon was quiet for a minute. "Is it serious?"

"Yes, it is." Miguel quickly went to get his keys from the kitchen while she talked on the phone. He wanted to hurry back to hear exactly what she was saying to Simon.

"Is it because of the distance with me living in Delaware?"

"No, it's not."

Simon pleaded! "Is it something that I did or didn't do? If it is, just tell me!"

Mackenzie walked out of the front door to have a little privacy. "Simon, it's nothing you did. You're a good person. It's just that I'm with someone else."

"Can we talk about this? Mackenzie, we've been seeing each other for about four months now."

"Yeah, but not exclusively. You were seeing other women too! Simon, I'm not trying to be rude or disrespectful, but it's late and I need to go. The time that we spent together was great and I'm glad that we hung out."

Simon sounded frantic! "Mackenzie, this can't be it! You can't do this to us!"

Mackenzie could feel herself getting upset. "Simon, you made it clear to me we were just friends *frequently*. So now that *I'm* with someone else, why are you having an issue?"

"What we had was more than just a friendship!"

"Simon, if we had more than just a friendship, we would have discussed that and made it known before today!" Simon didn't know what to say.

Miguel sped the process up a bit. He walked behind her and started kissing the back of her neck. "Babe, you ready to go?" Miguel made sure that his voice was loud enough for Simon to hear him.

Mackenzie tried to whisper, "Yeah, I'll be right there! Simon, I have to go."

"Is that him? Is he there with you?" Simon yelled.

Miguel heard him through the phone and made a funny face at Mackenzie, making her smile. He kissed her on the neck, making sure that Simon heard the smooching sound of his wet kiss. "Let's go!"

Simon heard everything. "Mackenzie, Mackenzie!"

Miguel kissed Mackenzie on the lips, took the phone away from her hands, and ended the call. "Let's go!"

~First week of August: Friday, the day of the NY trip~

As Mackenzie drove home from her aunt's house, she couldn't help but think of her mom. She missed her so much. Going to New York always seemed like going to a family reunion until her mom and dad died. Mackenzie pulled up to her house while making a mental list of the chores she had to do before they went to New York. As soon as she walked in the door, her house phone rang. Mackenzie closed the door behind her and picked up the cordless phone. "Hello?"

"Hi Mackenzie, it's Simon."

Mackenzie had a slight attitude. "Simon? What's up?"

Simon could hear the tension in her voice and tried to lighten up the surprising call. "How've you been?"

"Good, I'm on my way out of town."

"I'm going to be in Philly this weekend and I wanted to know if I could come by and talk to you."

"I'm sorry, I can't. I'll be out of town for the entire weekend!" Mackenzie said, trying to rush the call.

"To be honest with you, I'm already here in Philly. I can just come by real quick and we can talk outside at the park or on your step." Mackenzie felt a little strange. She walked over to her enclosed porch window and peeked to see if he was out there, and he was! Simon parked across the street from her house and was sitting on the driver's side of his black Lexus. She checked the time on the cordless phone. It was 6:24 and Miguel was coming to pick her up at seven. Mackenzie didn't want to call him because of his temper.

"Simon, I can't. I'm going away for the weekend. I'm leaving pretty soon, and I still have some things that I have to do before I go."

"Ok, when you come back, do you think we can talk a bit more?"

"Yeah, sure! Definitely!" Mackenzie replied, reassuring him that everything was cool.

"Ok, Mackenzie! I can't wait for us to talk!"

"Take care, Simon."

"You too, Mackenzie!"

Mackenzie went over to the window to make sure that he was leaving. About five minutes later, he pulled off. Mackenzie called Miguel, and he answered right away. "Hey babe, I'm on my way now to pick you up."

"Miguel."

Miguel could hear from the tone of her voice that something wasn't right. "What? What's wrong?"

"How much longer will it take for you to get here?"

"Ten minutes! Why, what's wrong?"

"I didn't want to call you because I didn't want you to be upset."

"Mackenzie, what happened?"

Mackenzie opened her door and scanned up and down the street. "Remember that guy Simon, who called me that night after you went to Vegas?"

"Yeah, what about him?"

Mackenzie closed the door and turned on the extra interior lock. "He called me on my house phone as soon as I got in the door." Miguel got quiet. "He wanted to know if we could talk some more. I told him I couldn't since I was going out of town. He said that he just wanted to talk outside on the step or at the park. When I peeked through the blinds, he was parked across the street. He left after I told him I couldn't."

"Are you packed yet?"

"Just about."

"Lock all the doors and finish packing. I'll be there soon."

"Alright bye."

Miguel just hung up the phone. Mackenzie ran upstairs, packed a few more items, and straightened up both her bedroom and bathroom. She walked downstairs and put her bags by the front door. Mackenzie sat down and tried to relax while waiting for Miguel. About ten minutes later, the doorbell rang. Mackenzie walked to the door. "Who is it?"

"It's me."

Mackenzie opened the door and Miguel kissed her. "You alright?"

"Yes, I'm just wondering why he's acting like this!"

"It's either because he can't have you and he cares about you or he's crazy. But I don't give a fuck why he's doing it! When you told him it was over, he shouldn't have called you anymore!" Miguel picked up her cordless phone and pressed a button to view Simon's information. He then opened his cell phone, sent a quick text, and put his phone in his pocket.

Mackenzie looked confused. "What are you doing?"

Miguel ignored her and hugged her tight. "Are you ready to go to NY or what?"

Mackenzie held on to his neck. "Yes, I am." She kissed his lips. "Thank you for being there for me!"

"That's what I'm supposed to do!"

"Miguel, I love you so much!"

"Let's get on the road! My grandma is cooking one of my favorites and I can't wait for you to meet her!"

"Well, let's go, son!" Miguel laughed at her funny New York accent and smacked her on the ass!

Chapter 8–Meeting the Fam.!

~ 9:38 p.m.~

Miguel was excited as he pulled up to his grandmother's house in Prospect Heights in Brooklyn. "We're here!" Mackenzie picked up her purse and got out of the car. The both of them stretched and walked up to the brownstone.

"Miguel? What about the bags?"

"We're not staying here!"

"Why not?"

He walked up closer to her. "You can't be making all that noise up in there! My grandma would kill me!" Mackenzie laughed and hit him on the shoulder!

Just then, Heather came to the door. "What's up Miguel!" She said, giving him an enormous hug, "And you must be Mackenzie! It's nice to meet you!" Heather smiled while hugging Mackenzie.

Mackenzie returned her warm embrace. "It's nice to meet you too!"

Heather was so happy! "Come on in!" Mackenzie stepped inside the house first, and about six different women were sitting on the couch in the living room. Heather walked ahead of Mackenzie and looked at the ladies. "Everybody, this is Mackenzie, my brother's fiancé!" The girls politely said hello and Mackenzie did the same.

Miguel stepped in and Mackenzie watched the girls gawking. "What's up Miguel?"

Another asked, "How have you been?"

Then another said, "Long time no see!"

Miguel nodded his head, "Hey what's up!" Mackenzie smiled at their immaturity! She simply chuckled and grinned at Miguel!

Heather put her hands on her hips and rolled her eyes at them! "Ladies, please save that shit for the men outside!" Her friends quickly left out to get dressed for the club while Heather ran up the stairs.

Miguel's grandmother sounded off in the distance! "Heather, you know I don't like cursing in my house unless I'm the one doing it!" Mackenzie walked into the kitchen and saw a small woman cooking over the stove. Mackenzie kept staring, thinking of her grandmother that had passed. His grandmother turned around and saw her standing there, staring. Miguel came up behind Mackenzie.

"Grandma!"

His grandmother gleamed! "Hey, sweetheart!" They hugged and gave each other kisses. "How was the drive, baby?"

"It was fine! Grandma, I want to…"

Miguel's grandmother didn't even let him finish his introduction. "Mackenzie, baby, come here, girl!"

Mackenzie smiled and walked over to her with open arms. "It's nice to meet you, Mrs. Joy!"

"It's wonderful to finally meet you! Oh, my goodness, you're beautiful!"

"Thank you!" Mackenzie said softly, while blushing.

Miguel laughed out loud. "So much for introductions!"

After washing their hands, all four of them sat down to eat dinner in the dining room. Mrs. Joy cooked fried chicken, string beans, macaroni and cheese, cornbread, steak, baked potatoes, and broccoli.

They all held hands while Mrs. Joy began the prayer. "Lord, we thank you this evening for allowing us to come together as a family once again with a new addition! We appreciate your everlasting love, kindness, and mercy. We humbly ask you to please bless this food that we are about to receive. We love you! We thank you, and we ask for all things in Jesus' name. Amen!"

"Amen!"

As soon as they began eating dinner, the interrogation process began, and Mrs. Joy went first! "So, Mackenzie, where are you from?"

"I grew up in Philly and then moved to New York. After college, I moved back to Philly!"

Mrs. Joy joked! "You didn't like NY enough to stay, huh? I can dig it!" Miguel paused for a moment because he knew Mackenzie was going to let her know why.

Mackenzie continued eating the delicious food while she explained. "No. It's just that my family moved to NY to take care of my grandmother while she was sick. When she died, we stayed here in New York. But when my parents died, I couldn't live in the house by myself."

Heather and Mrs. Joy stopped eating and just stared at Mackenzie. Heather slightly tilted her head toward the table while squinting her eyes, trying to grasp Mackenzie's circumstance. "So, your mom *and* dad died?"

Mackenzie could tell that they were really surprised. "Yes, while I was in college. After graduating, I moved back to Philly. My mom's sister helped me out a lot."

Mrs. Joy grasped her chest, understanding how difficult it must have been for her. "I'm sorry to hear that, baby."

"Yeah, me too! I miss them terribly, but they're in a better place, so it's ok."

Heather tried to lighten the mood. "What about brothers and sisters?"

"I am the only child. But I have loads of cousins!" Mackenzie ate more of her chicken and string beans. Miguel just listened while stuffing his face!

Heather changed her line of questioning and went for the gusto! "So, what do you do, Mackenzie?"

"I'm a therapist at the VA hospital in Philly."

"Do you like it?"

"Heather, I love it! You know, with my parents dying and having no siblings, loneliness creeps up often. But when you have a career or a hobby that allows you to pour out all of that compassion into something or someone else, it's not that bad! I'm helping a lot of veterans from Iraq, and they need a lot of attention. I'm glad that I have the time to give! It works out for all of us!" Mackenzie smiled at Miguel. He smiled right back at her and resumed eating.

Heather smiled and continued. "I hear you, Mackenzie! That's great! So, do you work Monday through Friday?"

Mackenzie felt the vibe and smiled. "No. I pretty much make up my own schedule."

Heather took a sip of her juice and looked at Mackenzie. "Oh, so you only work part-time?"

"Sometimes it feels that way! I have a lot of flexibility." Mackenzie ate the rest of her string beans and moved on to the macaroni and cheese. Miguel was surprised because he thought she worked full-time.

Heather was on a roll and kept on going! "So how do you make ends meet from working part-time?"

Miguel knew where she was headed! "Heather, calm down!" Despite feeling flustered by his confusion over Mackenzie's finances, he didn't want Heather to make Mackenzie feel unwelcome.

Mackenzie turned to Miguel and smiled. "It's ok! She's only looking out for you." Mrs. Joy turned to Miguel with a surprised smile on her face. "Heather, working for the government helps with insurance, paying for my utilities, and other things."

Heather was now wondering if she was a gold digger. "What about your rent, car note, and stuff?"

Mackenzie took another fork full of macaroni and cheese and tried to mind her manners! The food was unbelievably good! "My truck and house are both paid for," she replied before elegantly stuffing her mouth. Both Miguel and Mrs. Joy were now staring at Mackenzie, too! Mackenzie was tired of playing the guessing game, so she cut to the chase. "Heather, my parents weren't rich, but they were smart. They lived well, and they planned well. When they died, I was the sole beneficiary of their life insurance policies. That's why I choose to work part-time and why my house and truck are both paid for."

Heather felt bad about asking her all of those questions, but she felt compelled to! "Mackenzie, I wasn't trying to be mean. It's just that..."

"I understand, and it's ok! No love lost here!"

Heather stretched her arm out on the table and reached out to Mackenzie. "None here either!" Mackenzie took her hand and accepted her unspoken apology. Mrs. Joy just smiled at all of them.

Heather now moved to Miguel, who was shocked as hell! "So, Miguel, how does it feel knowing that your woman doesn't need you in the money department? Can you handle that?" Mackenzie started coughing a little from laughing!

Mrs. Joy grabbed Mackenzie's hand. "You ok, sweet child?"

"Yes, Mrs. Joy!"

Miguel stared at Mackenzie. "To be honest with you, I knew she worked at the VA, but I didn't know she worked part-time, because I never really asked! And I'm just learning about an inheritance!"

Heather clapped her hands loudly, trying to stir the pot! "Uh-Ohhh! Mackenzie, why didn't you tell him?"

Mackenzie tilted her head. "Money shouldn't matter, right? Besides, he found out when I was in a heated conversation with one of his associates in Florida."

Miguel dropped his fork on the table and turned all the way around so that he could see her dead on! "Mackenzie, you were serious when you told that to Yvonne?" Mrs. Joy and Heather cracked up laughing! Miguel thought that when Mackenzie was talking to Yvonne about her net worth, Mackenzie was making it all up!

"Would you love me any less if I said that I *was* lying in Florida?"

"No! But…"

Mackenzie kissed him on the cheek before he could finish what he was saying. "Ok."

Miguel's eyes were about to pop out of his head! "Mackenzie, do you have…"

"Miguel, I have enough to take care of myself. Besides, I'm sure you have a lot more than me anyway, so it doesn't even matter, right?"

"You're right!"

Mackenzie kissed him again and finished eating her food. Mrs. Joy knew what she did and admired her strength and ability to humble herself. She could also see that Mackenzie truly loved Miguel, and that she had a lot of money!

Mackenzie pointed to the last bit of macaroni and cheese with her fork! "Everything was so good Mrs. Joy!"

"Would you like some more, baby?"

"Yes, I would!"

Mackenzie stood up, and Miguel touched her arm. "Sit down, I'll get it!"

Mackenzie sat back down. "Thank you, Miguel! So, Heather, what are you doing for your birthday tomorrow?"

"I'm going out dancing with my girls and that's about it."

Miguel looked disgusted while fixing Mackenzie's plate. "Her man is so full of shit it's not even funny! He gets in an argument with her so that he doesn't have to buy her shit with his cheap ass!"

His grandmother raised her index finger. "Watch your mouth now!" She said, trying hard not to laugh. "You know what? I think he does it because he's not ready to commit."

Heather turned to Mackenzie. "What do you think?"

"What's going on?"

Heather leaned closer to her. "It's simple. Every year he does this on my birthday!"

Mackenzie thought for a moment. "Does he do it on Christmas?"

Miguel interjected! "Yup!"

"Shut up Miguel!" Heather shouted. Mrs. Joy shook her head, laughing, and agreeing with Miguel.

Mackenzie continued, "How long have the both of you been together?"

"Three years!"

Mackenzie squinted her eyes. "Heather, have you told him how you feel about him not coming through on those holidays?"

"Yes, I'm always telling him how I feel about it."

Mackenzie tried to get to the gist of Heather's issue. "So basically, you've communicated with him, and you've given him chances to straighten up."

"Yes!"

"Ok, so what do you think **you** should do?" Miguel made her plate and huffed out loud so that everyone could hear! Heather didn't know what to say. "Seriously speaking, Heather, you are a beautiful young woman. I don't understand the problem. Gifts aren't just about money, it's about selfless giving from one person to the other. If you've already communicated this to him and how important it is to you, and have given him a chance, it's now time to gather your energy and focus on what you need to do now. But you must also think about it from his point of view as well. If everything is all good for three hundred sixty-five days in the year, *minus* two or three days, why should he make any changes?"

Mackenzie continued, so that Heather could understand. "Are those days significant enough for you to end a three-year relationship with someone you care about?

Can you give him another chance? Relationships are hard to counsel because sometimes people don't want to talk about how they feel to someone they don't really know or trust. To be brutally honest with you, I could say leave him and your grandmother could say stay, but when it comes down to it, it's your choice! It's your life!"

Miguel handed Mackenzie her plate. "Thank You Miguel!"

Miguel poked his head in Heather's face! "Now, what are you going to do about that broke ass-mutha-fucka'!"

Mrs. Joy slammed her fist on the table! "Miguel!"

"Sorry, Grandma!" Miguel laughed while mouthing the same question to Heather silently!

Heather rolled her eyes at Miguel and stood up from the table. "Thanks, Mackenzie! I'm gonna get ready to go! Do you want to come along?"

Mackenzie politely smiled. "No thanks. Maybe we can hang out sometime tomorrow."

"Ok, that sounds good!" Heather hugged her and whispered in her ear, "Thanks for the advice."

Miguel hugged Heather! "Alright! Be careful!"

"Heather, call me tomorrow!" Mrs. Joy yelled.

Heather walked toward the front door and opened it. "See y'all tomorrow!"

"Bye," they all yelled in unison!

Mackenzie ate up the rest of her string beans. "Mrs. Joy, your cooking reminds me so much of my grandmother's cooking."

"Where in New York did your grandmother live?"

"Over in Bed-Stuy!"

"Get out of here! So, who lives there now?"

Mackenzie kept on eating! "Nobody! When I'm visiting friends here in New York, I stay there."

Mrs. Joy got up from the table. "Do you all want some dessert?"

Miguel raised his hand as if he was still in elementary school. "You know I do, grandma!"

Mackenzie laughed, seeing how Miguel was so at ease. "I'll have some too! Miguel, where is the bathroom?"

"Just go upstairs, turn to…"

Mrs. Joy quickly turned to Miguel. "Miguel, take her on up there now!" Miguel laughed and took her hand as they walked up the stairs toward the bathroom. Mackenzie went in and Miguel followed right behind her. Miguel pushed up against her body and grabbed her breasts.

Mackenzie playfully smacked his hands away! "You better go downstairs before you get us in trouble!"

"Mackenzie, what you have or don't have, it doesn't matter to me, ok? I love you all the same."

She closed the door a little and started kissing his neck. "So, even if I was a millionaire or if I needed a couple of dollars, it doesn't matter?"

"No."

"Good, because I need to borrow a couple dollas' to buy one of those New York hot dogs!" Miguel laughed and kissed her.

Mackenzie tenderly caressed his face. "I didn't embarrass you, did I?"

"No! Don't say stuff like that! You were being you!"

Mackenzie nodded her head and took a deep breath, feeling at ease. "Where are we staying tonight?"

"I got a room at a hotel."

"Do you want to stay at my house instead? That way, we won't be that far, and you don't have to pay!"

Miguel stared right back at her. "Are you sure you want to stay there?"

"Yeah, it's not haunted or anything!"

"Ok, I'll cancel the reservation." She kissed him and then again on his neck. Miguel pulled on her shorts.

"Miguel we can't! Stop!"

"Just a little!"

Mackenzie smacked his hand away and kissed him. "Your grandma is downstairs waiting for us!"

"Well, we gotta go!"

They were both laughing like teenagers! Mackenzie tried to whisper, "We need to eat dessert first! You can wait until we get to the house, right?"

"No, not really! But ok!" Mackenzie kissed Miguel on his way out of the bathroom and closed the door.

Miguel ran down the steps and sat down at the table with his grandma. She could practically see the happiness secreting from each pore in his body! "How do you feel about her, Miguel?"

"Grandma, I love her to death! She's smart, caring, beautiful, and I can talk to her about anything!"

Mrs. Joy sat down, put her hands on the table, and stared at Miguel. "Did you tell her about Tamara and the baby?"

"Yeah, she knows."

"How did she react when you told her what Tamara was trying to do?"

Miguel took a sip of his water and wiped his mouth with his cloth napkin. "She was upset and said she would never do anything like that to me."

Mrs. Joy crossed her arms in front of her chest and sat back in her chair. "What about what you're doing? Does she know that?" Mackenzie could hear them talking as she tiptoed down the stairs.

"Grandma, I'm gonna…"

Mrs. Joy was mad as hell. "You gonna do what, Miguel? Are you gonna tell her you launder money for drug dealers and killers? Do you think she's gonna want to be with you after learning about *that*? You need to stop doing that shit and be more responsible, especially if…"

Mackenzie strolled in and folded her arms in front of her chest while standing in the doorway. "Miguel, is that true?"

Miguel turned toward the doorway, startled! "Mackenzie…"

"Is it true?" Mackenzie asked angrily.

"Mackenzie, I was gonna' tell you."

"Ok! *Now* can you explain!"

Miguel's grandmother started laughing and hit the table with her hand. "I want to hear this shit! I ain't going nowhere either! It's been a **long-time** coming honey!"

Miguel frowned his face at his grandmother and then to Mackenzie! "Can we talk about this later?"

"No! I think we should talk about it now!"

Miguel took a deep breath and let it out through his nose. He stood up from the table and walked over to Mackenzie. "I used to sell drugs years ago. I stopped selling drugs and started helping people wash the money they got from selling drugs."

Mackenzie rubbed her forehead and paced the floor. "Why haven't you stopped? You have a house, a car, and bikes! Why haven't you stopped?"

"I was trying to get some more money saved up and then I was going to stop!"

Mackenzie recognized the behavior he was exhibiting. "How much money are you trying to save?"

"I was going for two million and I got it. I just want to get to three and then I'm done!"

Mackenzie closed her eyes and pinched her eyebrows together. "What if I told you I don't want you to do that anymore?"

"After I get to three, I'm going to stop!"

Mrs. Joy couldn't help herself! She had to interject! "Mackenzie, he told me the *same shit* years ago!"

Mackenzie placed her arms behind her back like a soldier. "Miguel, you have two million dollars. Does money mean that much to you?"

"Damn it, Mackenzie! It's about security!" Miguel yelled.

"You know what? I think you're right! We should talk about this somewhere else." Mackenzie grabbed her purse. "It was nice to meet you, Mrs. Joy."

"Nice to meet you too!" Mackenzie walked out of the house and Miguel followed, not saying anything to his grandmother.

Miguel drove to The Brooklyn Bridge Park so that they could talk. As soon as he put the car in park, Mackenzie got out of the car and started yelling, "Miguel, you should have told me! Why didn't you tell me?"

Miguel spoke in a low tone, trying to calm her down. "Mackenzie, I was gonna tell you. I just didn't know how, and there was never a good time to tell you."

"That's bullshit! I can't go through this shit with you!" Mackenzie started tearing up. "I love you and if we are going to be together, you gotta stop!" Miguel was stunned at how upset she was. Most women didn't care about where the money was coming from, just as long as they kept getting whatever he gave to them. He wasn't prepared for this and couldn't help but stare at her while she cried. "I can't lose you too!"

Miguel held her in his arms. "I'm sorry, baby."

Mackenzie pushed him away. "You're sorry! You're fucking sorry? I told you about my family dying in a car crash and you're in the streets gambling with your life while trying to build one with me? And you're sorry?" Mackenzie walked over to the water and cried even harder. "I fuckin' knew it! I knew this was too good to be fuckin' true!"

Miguel walked over to her and touched her arm. "You're not gonna lose me."

"Miguel cut the bullshit, ok! Just stop it!" Mackenzie wiped her face and took a couple of breaths while her head was in her hands. She picked her head up and put her hands on his chest. "Miguel, I love you and I want to be with you. I cannot be with you in any type of way until you have stopped. I'm sorry!"

Miguel put his hands on her arms. "You won't lose me, baby! Ever! Give me some time!" She shook her head no while still crying and walking toward the water. Miguel walked over to her. "Ok! October, your birthday... I'll stop in October! I promise you! I promise!" He went to kiss her, but she turned and walked away. Miguel went up to her again from behind and held her. Tears were steadily falling down Mackenzie's eyes. Miguel turned her around. He couldn't console her with his words and felt defeated. Miguel yelled! "Mackenzie, please just stop!"

Mackenzie started shouting uncontrollably! "I don't want to lose you over some fuckin' money! It's not worth it! I want to be with you, not be with you while you're sitting in fuckin' jail or dead!"

"Mackenzie, I'm gonna stop!"

Mackenzie picked up a rock and threw it out at the water angrily! "Then stop now! Stop right now! Show someone else how to do what you do and stop!" Miguel was quiet, but Mackenzie was livid! "The girls you were fuckin' with, they *like* that steady flow of cash, huh? They care more about the fuckin' money than **you**! Here I come wanting nothing but the *best* for you and you can't understand why I'm crying and acting like this as if **I'm** the fucked up one! Your ex who was pregnant, did she know?"

"Yeah."

"That's why she was with you in the first fuckin' place, huh?" Miguel didn't say anything. Mackenzie stood facing the water and tried to calm down. She didn't want to go down that road knowing how much it hurt him. Mackenzie wiped her face with her shirt and just continued breathing.

Miguel contemplated what she had expressed to him. He could see her wiping her eyes and felt terrible. Miguel went over to her. "Mackenzie, I'm gonna make it right! Just give me a chance! I promise! Just give me until October!"

Mackenzie's eyes were focused on the water. "I can't be with you, Miguel."

"Yes, you can!" Mackenzie shook her head no. Miguel pulled her to him and kissed her lips. "I love you. Be with me and wait for me!"

"No. I can't do that."

"Yes, you can! Stop saying that you can't!" Mackenzie started crying again. "Be with me, baby. Just give me until October! You know I love you!" He kissed her again and held her close. "Mackenzie, give me a chance." Mackenzie's tears kept flowing and Miguel wiped them away. "Don't cry. I'll make it all better. I promise!" Miguel kissed her again and walked her to the car.

They left the park and went to Mackenzie's house. Mackenzie unlocked the door while Miguel brought in their bags. She walked toward the kitchen and Miguel kissed her. He didn't feel her responding to him. "What's wrong?"

"I love you too much to leave." Miguel walked up to her close and kissed her. He pulled her shorts down and she took his pants off as well. She took his hand, walked upstairs to the front bedroom, and laid down on her back. Mackenzie took off her shirt, showing her wine-colored satin bra.

Miguel tried to solidify his promise. "Let's make a deal! On your birthday, I'm going to stop. Then I'm going to take you away for two weeks to anywhere you want to go."

"Do you promise that you'll stop on my birthday?"

"Yes!" Miguel said, kissing and sucking all over her neck. He squeezed her breasts and softly bit her nipples through her bra. Mackenzie pulled his shirt over his head. Miguel took over and pulled down his underwear, along with everything else. After taking her thong off, Mackenzie quickly sat up and began sucking his dick. "Damn Mackenzie! Suck it, baby!"

Mackenzie went to work slobbering all over him! "Promise me!"

"I promise! Baby, I promise!" She stopped and laid back on the bed. He laid on top of her and kissed her. Miguel put his dick inside her and began making love to her.

"Miguel, stop for a minute!"

"Why?"

"Please stop!"

Miguel stopped! "What's wrong, baby?"

"Miguel, stop coming in me!"

"I thought we already talked about that, Mackenzie!"

He started moving again. "Miguel you can't! I'm serious!"
Miguel ignored her and kept on going for a while! Mackenzie
moaned and begged him to go deeper.

"Are you ready?"

"No Miguel!"

"Yes, you are! Tell me you want it!"

"Miguel! Oh my God! Please! You're gonna get me
pregnant!"

"I know!" He grabbed her hips and moved deeper inside of her! As he shot his come inside of her, she moaned and climaxed right along with him.

~ Saturday morning ~

Mackenzie woke up and took a quick shower. When she got out of the shower, she peeked in on Miguel. He was still asleep. Mackenzie oiled her body and put on a tee shirt, some boy short panties, and jean shorts. She grabbed her bag, his car keys, and drove to the store to buy groceries and snacks. Twenty minutes later, she drove straight home. Mackenzie walked upstairs to see that Miguel was still sound asleep. After tiptoeing downstairs, she began to prepare breakfast. Mackenzie's phone vibrated while she whisked the eggs. "Hello!"

Tommy yelled all the way through the phone! "Hey, honey!"

"Hey, Tommy! How are you?"

"I'm good. Where are you?"

Mackenzie stopped whisking and laughed! "I'm in New York! Where are you?"

"My ass is here to girl!"

"Are you following me, Tommy?" Mackenzie said, laughing!

"Yeah, I'm stalking your ass! Like I ain't got shit else to do!"

"Are you here by yourself or with Mr. Starks?"

"You know his ass can't go nowhere without his boo! Where is the Beast?"

"In bed sleeping!"

Tommy snapped his fingers! "That's right girl! Work that dick 'til his ass is comatose." They both laughed up a storm! "So, are we on for shopping?"

Mackenzie viewed the time on the stove. "What time do you want to go?"

"Let's say around 12:30ish, 1ish!"

"I'll send you a text to confirm and we'll hook up from there."

"Alright baby, I'll talk to you later!"

Mackenzie blew her a kiss over the phone. "I love you girl!"

"Love you too! Smooches!"

Mackenzie put the turkey bacon and sausage in the oven so they would stay warm. The grits were nice and smooth, and the biscuits were done. She buttered the biscuits and prepared the pan for the eggs with melted butter.

Mackenzie took her time and set the table like her grandmother and mother used to. She set up the plates, forks, and glasses. While scrambling the eggs, Mackenzie felt so elated and complete that she wanted to scream. The eggs were done, so she removed them from the eye on the stove.

Mackenzie wiped her hands and made her way upstairs when she heard her cell phone vibrating. She picked it up and Wayne's name appeared. Mackenzie sent it to voicemail and seriously thought about changing her number. As she walked up the stairs, she could hear the water running. Mackenzie stood in the bathroom doorway while Miguel finished brushing his teeth. "Good morning Mr. Conway!"

"Hey baby, come here!"

Mackenzie went over to him and kissed him on the lips. "It's time to eat breakfast!"

"Ok baby, I'll be right down." As she walked away, he smacked her butt!

Mackenzie fixed their plates and took out the juice from the fridge. She waited for a couple of minutes, then went back upstairs. He was on the bed talking on the phone. "Miguel?"

"I'll be right there, baby!" Mackenzie went back downstairs and put butter on their grits.

Seconds later, Miguel walked into the kitchen and smiled at how beautifully she set the kitchen table. "Baby, this looks so good!" He sat down and they prayed over the food.

Mackenzie got up and brought the jelly out for the biscuits. "So, what's the plan for the day?"

Miguel stuffed his mouth! "I was going to take my sister out to lunch and buy her something that she wanted for her birthday."

"That sounds cool! While y'all are out, I'll go out with Tommy."

Miguel instantly stopped chewing. "He's here?"

"Yeah, he called me this morning! I told him I would let him know if I was going out with him or not! What about later on tonight?"

Miguel tweaked his watch. "I have something I need to do while I'm here. But it won't take me long." Mackenzie smiled and kept on eating. "Mackenzie, it's not going to take me long at all!"

"Miguel, you know I'm not concerned with the time. Let's just enjoy our breakfast and the rest of the day."

~

Mackenzie sent Tommy a text message while she was getting her clothes together for the day. Tommy sent her a quick text that he was on his way. Heather was also on her way to Mackenzie's to meet up with Miguel. Mackenzie put on her sexy pink sundress, carried her pink clutch-purse, and wore pink sandals to match. She had her hair down, with very little make-up.

Miguel had a frown on his face! "Damn! Where else are you going?"

Mackenzie laughed! "Anywhere I want to!"

"Don't get smart! You better be careful and call me."

The doorbell rang and Miguel went downstairs to the door and opened it. "Hey! Happy birthday!" Miguel said, hugging Heather.

"Thank you!"

Mackenzie walked down the stairs and joined in! "Happy birthday Heather!" She walked over to Heather and hugged her!

"Thank you, Mackenzie! And where are *you* going dressed like that?"

"Well, while Miguel is taking you out for your birthday, one of my close friends, who is up from Florida for the weekend, is taking me shopping. She should be here any minute! Where are you all headed out to?"

Miguel tapped Heather's shoulder. "Yeah, where do you wanna go?"

"I …" Heather stopped mid-sentence as they all heard loud music coming from a car driving down the street. The car was playing Biance's "Single Ladies" loud and clear! Mackenzie smiled and went to open the front door. Tommy was driving a red Ferrari 612 Scaglietti. Miguel and Heather were standing right behind Mackenzie.

Heather couldn't help her eyes from popping out of her head! "Damn!" Miguel heard Heather's astonishment! She shrugged her shoulders apologetically.

Tommy double-parked, making sure other cars could get by, and got out of the car. He had on a red polo short-sleeve shirt, blue jeans, and some red canvas polo sneakers.

He walked up to the porch smiling from ear to ear! "M & M, what's happening, kids?"

"Hey, Tommy!" Mackenzie and Miguel said.

Mackenzie gave him a big hug. "I can't believe you're here!"

"Me either, honey!" Tommy pointed to Heather. "And who is this young diva to be?" Heather cracked up laughing!

Mackenzie gave the introduction! "Tommy, this is Heather! Miguel's *one and only* sister!"

Tommy put his hand up to his mouth, showing just how surprised he was to hear the news! "What?! No sisters? Well, Ms. Heather, have you ever had an all-out day?"

Heather shook her head no while quickly glancing at Miguel and Mackenzie. "No, what is that?"

Mackenzie turned toward Heather and was about to explain, but Tommy kindly took over. "Ms. Heather, an all-out day is a day where you go *all-the-hell-out*! Mackenzie, you need to tell her how we roll, baby!" Tommy demanded while snapping his fingers.

Mackenzie didn't want to throw a wrench in Miguel's plans with Heather. "Tommy, today is her birthday! Miguel is taking her out to lunch and to do some shopping!"

Tommy shook his head no! "Mackenzie, you are such a considerate sweetheart! That's one of the reasons why I love you so, but I must insist." Tommy looked at Heather. "Honey, how old are you today?"

Heather smiled excitedly, "I'm 23."

Tommy eyeballed Miguel. "Miguel, I know this is your *only* sister, but she is at one of the most important turning points in her life. You must let us do what we do best and *BAAH-RING* your sister into diva-hood correctly!"

Miguel laughed and turned to Heather. "What do you want to do?"

"I want to go, but I still want to go out to eat with you!"

"Ok, call me when you all are done so I can pick you up! Mackenzie, I'm going to take care of that business while y'all are out, ok?"

Mackenzie politely smiled and kissed Miguel. "Ok."

Tommy was already walking and talking to Heather on the way to the car. Miguel and Mackenzie were still on the porch talking. Mackenzie placed her arms around Miguel's neck. "Miguel, I love you."

"I love you too!"

Mackenzie winked her eye at him. "I have a surprise for you!"

Miguel kissed her lips again. "I have one for you too!"

Mackenzie nodded her head toward the house. "There is a second set of keys inside the end table, by the window in the living room. That's your set!"

"Oh, you're giving me keys, huh?" Mackenzie just winked at him and gave him another kiss.

Tommy started clapping his hands to get their attention! "Excuse me M&M's! Save it for the bedroom! Now, you must separate people! We have stores to explore and a whole lotta shit to buy!" Heather laughed while Mackenzie and Miguel smiled.

Miguel put his hand inside his pocket. Mackenzie quickly grabbed his hand. "Don't even think about it! I love you for *you*, not your pockets!" She walked away and switched her ass on the way to the car! Miguel took a deep breath and tried to smile despite his discontent.

Tommy shouted out in the street! "That's right! Shake it, girl! Miguel, you will **get no** better than that one right there, ok! So, you better get on board quick, honey!" Mackenzie kept strutting her stuff on the way to the car.

Miguel's fake smile faded. "I'm on my way, Tommy," he replied.

Tommy turned on the car and increased the volume on Beyonce's "Single Ladies". "You better hurry, son! The other shoppers are getting in line and I'm quite damn sure they want to buy! Miguel, honey, let me tell you something ok? They were all over her in Florida!"

Mackenzie playfully slapped Tommy's arm and yelled, "Shut up, Tommy!"

Tommy rolled his eyes at Mackenzie and pointed at Miguel while turning down the music! "Listen, I had to **act straight** just to keep them away! It was horrible! **Horr-i-bull**!"

"Tommy, be quiet and let's go!" Mackenzie said as she got settled inside the car. She yelled to Miguel, "She's only joking, baby!"

Tommy shook his head! "No, the hell I'm not! Mackenzie, why you lyin'? Girl, he needs to know the truth honey and I am **not** acting straight today for you or nobody else! No, no, no! I'm sorry!" Tommy waved her finger at Miguel! "Her fine scrumptious ass needs a ring so these men can stop harassing her beautiful self!"

Mackenzie slapped Tommy again on the arm and waved her hand at Miguel! "Miguel don't pay her any mind! Heather, she is a mess!" Heather was having a ball, laughing her head off.

Miguel stared at them, knowing what Tommy was saying was the truth. "Tommy, hold it down for me!"

Tommy gave Miguel a thumbs up! "Alright! Call Heather in about three hours! The women are out!" Tommy blasted Biance's "Single Ladies" again. "You hear that, Miguel! Tick-Tock, Tick-Tock! You don't want her singing this song to *you*! You better get on board and put a ring on it honey, and fast!"

"Would you just drive?" Mackenzie said, laughing.

"It's Heather's birthday! Yah- Hoo!" All the girls wailed down the street, singing and laughing. Miguel shook his head and knew what he had to do. He set his plan in motion.

Part 2: Coming Pronto!

www.ingramcontent.com/pod-product-compliance
Lightning Source LLC
Chambersburg PA
CBHW080724020726
47503CB00010B/2783